"Are you quite su... ..., Uncle Oliver?"

"Bless you boy, 'is 'ead ain't that 'ard."

The words swam into Lucas Bardine's consciousness on a wave of agony. His head was hurting dreadfully. Yet, still he had the presence of mind to stifle a groan as the conversation in the darkness above him continued.

"Did I not tell you that the letter would fetch him?" It was Stephen speaking. "He has a soft heart and a weak brain under all that blubber. He is a mass of sentiment is my dear cousin Lucas. I have known him to weep over a sad song ... so how could a mother's plight fail to move him?"

"Cor, 'e's awake."

In the glow from a small lighted candle, Lucas Bardine glimpsed his cousin Stephen's gloating eyes and the rugged face of the man with him. Then, he saw the cudgel descending. He tried to move his head out of the way but to no avail. He knew another moment of blinding agony again, then darkness blotted out everything.

"Maybe we ought to kill 'im," the man called Oliver said.

"No," Stephen smiled down at his cousin's recumbent form. "Let him live. Let him sweat and suffer a little before he dies . . ."

Stephen Bardine had made a deadly mistake in choosing to let Lucas live . . . and suffer. For a man can endure much when he lives for vengeance . . . and dreams of a beautiful woman.

Other Novels by Zabrina Faire

Lady Blue
The Midnight Match
The Romany Rebel
Enchanting Jenny

Published by
WARNER BOOKS

Your Warner Library of Regency Romance

The Wicked Cousin

Zabrina Faire

WARNER BOOKS

A Warner Communications Company

WARNER BOOKS EDITION

Copyright © 1980 by Florence Stevenson
All rights reserved.

ISBN: 0-446-94104-2

Cover art by Walter Popp

Warner Books, Inc., 75 Rockefeller Plaza, New York, N.Y.
10019

 A Warner Communications Company

Printed in the United States of America

First Printed: March, 1980

10 9 8 7 6 5 4 3 2 1

THE WICKED COUSIN

ONE

"April . . . oh, it is April and it really does look like it should look this morning!" So saying, Miss Bryony de Beaufre flung wide the windows of her chamber and glanced down on Duke Street, but finding nothing in its crowded length to please her poetic soul, she lifted her eyes toward a sky which had only the barest tracery of clouds in it and none of them near the sun. "It is," she continued, "a day just as I hoped it would be."

Mary Appleby, her maid, who stood a few paces away from her with comb in hand, looked at her aggrievedly. "Oh, Miss, your 'air be all a-fly an' I've but fixed it."

"Mary, Mary, do not grumble," Miss de Beaufre begged. "Have you ever seen the sky so blue? It should be lovely in the Park! 'Sweet spring, full of sweet days and roses!' I wish I might versify like George Herbert."

"If I might say so, Miss—" Mary spoke respectfully, yet with the authority of one who was fully six months older than her mistress—"gentlemen do not care for bluestockings."

"Mary!" Bryony laughed. "You do sound like Mama and I shall tell you as I tell her that I cannot quell my Muse, I must write. But is it not a lovely day? I was so afraid that it might rain and I should not be able to go driving with my Cousin Lucas."

"Oh, 'im," Mary muttered under her breath. She knew her mistress had a distinct partiality for the gentleman in question, though she herself could not understand why, not with all the handsome young bucks who were pursuing Bryony. She glanced proudly around the chamber. She had had to instruct Peggy, the housemaid, to bring in six extra vases to accomodate the flowers that had been sent this morning. It had been that way ever since Miss de Beaufre had arrived from the country. In fact, she had enjoyed an especial, if questionable, triumph by being voted an Incomparable by the dandies who sat in the bow window at Whites. Though Lady Honoria, her mother, had decried this particular encomium, Mary knew that she was also pleased that her daughter had created such a sensation. The maid glanced at the girl admiringly. Her modish blue gown brought out her coloring—Mary much preferred Miss de Beaufre's gold-shot chestnut curls and deep violet eyes to that type known as the "English rose." Her features were lovely—a straight little nose, a full mouth and the suspicion of a cleft in her pointed chin were augmented by the sparkle in her large eyes. She looked as if she loved life and indeed, she did. However, Mary wished that her mistress would sit still and not go bouncing around the room in so hoydenish a manner. "Miss," she begged in long-suffering tones, "do sit down."

"Oh, very well, Mary," Bryony sighed, submitting once more to her maid's ministrations. Her glance fell on the clock that stood on her mantelpiece, "Ah, it's nearly eleven and Lucas must come soon!"

Mary nodded and began to arrange Byrony's hair, wondering a second time why her mistress must be so excited over the arrival of a mere cousin, especially one like Mr. Lucas Bardine.

That this was a thought shared by Miss de Beaufre's mama was evident soon after Bryony had entered the white-and-gold drawing room where her ladyship was ensconced upon the graceful French chaise longue which she was wont to describe as "my bed of pain."

It was unfortunate that Lady Honoria should choose to sit not far from the Romney portrait depicting her as Persephone, commissioned by the late Sir Anthony de Beaufre some seventeen years earlier. In those days, she had resembled a nymph, her complexion being fair, her hair a ripe gold and her eyes a sparkling blue. However, a series of miscarriages, augmented by grief over her husband's death four summers ago, had rendered her old beyond her thirty-nine years. In the light that Bryony had praised, Lady Honoria looked shockingly yellow and wrinkled, and as her daughter approached her, she said querulously, "Bryony, do draw the curtains."

"Very well, Mama." Bryony obeyed and came to sit beside her parent. "I do hope you are not starting another of your headaches?"

"I am afraid I am, but never mind that. Why are you wearing your newest gown merely to go driving with Lucas?"

9

"Lucas likes me in blue."

"You have other blue gowns, and why are you sitting with your hands clasped about your knees?"

"It's comfortable," Bryony sighed, quickly changing her position.

"It is not ladylike. I do wish you would acquire some dignity. You are, after all, within two months of your eighteenth birthday and a recognized Incomparable."

"I thought you did not approve of that, Mama."

"I do not. You should not have your name bandied about all over town, but since it is, it behooves you to act in an adult manner . . . and, in a sense, it is very flattering."

"It is flattery I could do without, Mama. It is so constricting!" Bryony rolled her eyes upward and sighed. "I may not even smile at a gentleman without his thinking he has made a conquest, and if I waltz with the same partner twice, all those old tabbies at Almack's are sure he has made an offer and I have accepted. I am glad I shall be with Lucas this morning. He is so safe." Then, in a tone alternating between hope and resignation, she added, "I pray that the treatments he has taken in Brighton have helped."

Lady Honoria said disparagingly, "I cannot imagine that we shall see any change in a mere fortnight. I had thought he meant to stay much longer. I wonder what has brought him back to town so soon?"

"Has it been only a fortnight?" Bryony's expressive eyes widened. "It has seemed so very much longer to me."

"Really!" Lady Honoria's laugh was more than a shade derisive. "One would think you had a *tendresse* for Lucas."

"I do love him," she said positively. "He is the kindest man alive. Think what he has done for Cousin Stephen, bringing him out of nowhere and reinstating him with Great-Grandfather Bertram."

"Yes, one must admit that that was kind," Lady Honoria allowed. A small smile played about her colorless lips but was gone as she bent a censorious gaze upon her daughter's face. "When you say you love him, I pray you are using the term in a cousinly way. There's been no understanding between you, I hope."

"Understanding!" Bryony echoed incredulously. Then much to her mother's relief, she burst into laughter, "Oh, dear, I do wish Lucas could hear you! He would be as amused as I am."

"Well," her mother said, "I am glad of that, else I should have thought you'd taken leave of your senses."

A small spark flickered briefly in Bryony's eyes. Though she was well aware that Lady Honoria's attitude toward Lucas Bardine was similar to that of most of the *ton*, with the possible exception of the Prince Regent—who had reason to, and did, sympathize with him—she was annoyed. It occurred to her that she wished she might be able to tell her mother that she did indeed have a secret understanding with him. But to confess to a nonexistent passion for her second cousin would have given rise to serious complications, which would not only have hurt his feelings but would have cut her off from the enjoyment of a friendship she valued above all others. Since Bardine Court lay within walking distance of De Beaufre Abbey, outside of Bridgnorth on the Severn in Shropshire, and since Lady Honoria, as the child of Sir Bertram Bardine's eldest daughter Benecia, was the niece of Mr. Austin Bardine, Lucas's father, the families had always been very close. Bryony, in fact, had come to look upon Lucas as the brother she had never had, while he, seven years her senior, regarded her as his little sister; for he too was an only child. Yet unlike a real brother, he had never been nasty or teasing but always kind and unfailingly good-natured, qualities he had never lost, not even in the face of the cruel gibes which had invariably been his portion.

She smiled ruefully and, in the next moment, sighed smilingly, hoping that he had enjoyed at least a little success in Brighton, but though she never would have confessed it to her mama, she feared it was only one more stop in his eternal but unsuccessful quest to rid himself of the girth which had made him a laughing-stock all his life.

While these thoughts passed through Byrony's mind, Lady Honoria was regarding her daughter's lovely face with a large measure of exasperation. Unlike Bryony, she thought that the two weeks Mr. Bardine had spent in Brighton had passed far too quickly. Not for the first time, she wondered how a young female, who was fast becoming the toast of the town, could refuse all the flattering invitations she had received for that morning merely to be with her cousin. Though Sir Anthony had always disagreed with her, in her opinion it was a most disastrous association. While Lucas Bardine was quite as kind as Bryony insisted, and responsible for bringing that utterly charming and handsome young man she was already calling "dearest Stephen" into their immediate circle, Lady Honoria knew that rather than listening to her own dicta concerning the eligibility of the gentlemen who pursued her, Bryony invariably relied on Mr Bardine's advice. She frowned. It had been solely at his instigation, she knew, that her daughter had refused to encourage the Marquis of Montmere and the extremely wealthy young Mr. Nettleshield, both of whom came from fine families.

Furthermore, she feared that though Mr. Bardine had disclaimed interest in all females, his affection for Bryony might possibly exceed that of a mere friend, thus rendering his advice on matters matrimonial highly suspect.

There was a light tap on the drawing room doors. Both ladies looked up, knowing that Darby, the butler, was about to announce Mr. Lucas Bardine. As this knowledge entered their minds, their reception of it was almost ludicrously dissimilar—one face being bright with anticipation and the other dimmed with apprehension.

"Yes," Lady Honoria called in a resigned voice.

Darby, a thin, middle-aged man, was careful to throw open both doors as he intoned, "Mr. Lucas Bardine." He stepped back with almost indecent haste as if, Bryony thought watching the maneuver with some indignation, he were afraid of being trampled. Then as her cousin loomed over the threshold, she bit down a gasp of dismay, while her mother carefully concealed a smile of relief as she decided her recent fears were quite unfounded. Certainly, the said Mr. Lucas Bardine could, in no way, be considered a threat to a mother's peace of mind. Easily over six feet in height, he was, she decided happily, nearly as broad as he was tall.

Looking at her cousin, Bryony feared that his formidable bulk had, if anything, increased! Possibly, she thought hopefully, that impression was partially based on the fact that the styles of the day, so eminently becoming to a slim Beau Brummell, merely looked ludicrous on a man whose belly was so huge that she doubted he could see his feet. She was also unhappily sure that his valet must use twice the normal amount of muslin to wind his cravat about his thick neck and supposed it must lie uncomfortably against his several chins. His cheeks, she noted, had swelled so that eyes, nose and mouth looked very small. Yet, had his features not been so distorted by his great accumulation of poundage, she was of the opinion that they might have been pleasant, for both his parents had been handsome people. It might have been his mother's fault that he had grown so large; for, being the one surviving son of an inconsolable widow, his every wish had been indulged, and he had always liked his food.

"Ah, Lucas my dear." Lady Honoria found that she could speak with complete sincerity as she said, "How very pleasant to see you again."

"Pleasant for me, too, Cousin Honoria," he smiled, moving ponderously across the room to kiss her hand. "Hope you are in good health?" His habit of abbreviating his sentences stemmed, she knew, from lack of breath rather than from affectation.

"I am as well as might be expected," she told him with one of her frequent sighs. She was just about to launch into an interesting description of the various symptoms that had racked her in his absence when she saw, to her annoyance, that he was not attending. His eyes had wandered toward her daughter.

"How fares the Incomparable?" he asked as he bent over her hand.

"Lucas!" She glared at him. "I will thank you not to address me in that ridiculous manner!"

Lady Honoria shot her a reproving look. "I fear she has no appreciation of the honor bestowed upon her by the dandies."

Bryony, giving her mother a quelling glance, smiled up at her cousin and asked, "Have you brought your greys?"

"Chestnuts," he corrected.

"New?" she asked excitedly.

14

He nodded. "Purchased at Tattersall's, just before going to Brighton. Fine pair of high-steppers."

"Please sit down, Lucas," Lady Honoria invited, exhaling a sigh of relief as he chose a sturdy bench in preference to one of her spindly French chairs. "Did you enjoy Brighton?"

"Didn't go to enjoy it, Cousin Honoria, went for a purpose," he said. "Couldn't carry out plan—aversion for sea water."

"Oh, dear," Bryony exclaimed. "That time you almost drowned in that squall off the Irish coast—I'd forgotten that."

"I, too," he said. "All came back to me, moment I saw waves breaking on the shore."

"You could not have remained in Brighton long then," Lady Honoria said.

"No," he admitted ruefully. "Went back to the Court."

"Oh," Bryony nodded and knew immediately why his weight had increased. He was much beloved in his household and she was sure that Mrs. Griffith, the cook, must have outdone herself in preparing all the viands he loved. "You spent most of your time at the Court then?"

"Did." He nodded.

"Did you ride over to the Eaves and visit with Grandfather?" Lady Honoria asked.

"Once. Not up to snuff, poor man."

"Nothing dangerous, I hope," Lady Honoria said.

"Shouldn't think so. Given to refining on health a bit too much. Runs in family, should think."

Bryony, seeing a look of indignation in her parent's faded blue eyes, said quickly, "Lucas, dear, do take me driving."

"Bryony!" her mother protested. "Dear Lucas has only just arrived."

"He has arrived to take me driving," Bryony pointed out punctiliously, "and I do not see why we must needs sit here, exchanging all this inconsequential chatter."

"Bryony, you are much too impetuous," Lady Honoria chided. Turning to Mr. Bardine, she added, "I do hope you will forgive her."

"Nothing to forgive, Cousin," he said, his eyes dwelling fondly on Bryony. There was a note in his voice that caused Lady Honoria to look at him sharply but, as usual, his expression was not decipherable amidst the rolls of flesh that bloated his countenance.

"That is absolutely true," Bryony agreed. "There's no reason for Lucas to forgive me. Certainly I need not stand on ceremony with him, Mama."

"It is good practice for you to stand on ceremony with everyone, my dear, and remember that you are no longer . . ."

"A hoyden, but a young lady," Bryony finished lightly. She winked at Mr. Bardine. "But I will never need to be a young lady with Lucas, will I?"

"Assuredly not. If you're ready, shall be delighted to take you driving." he said.

"I have been ready all morning," Bryony told him, drawing another pained glance from her mama.

"If I were you, Lucas," Lady Honoria said shortly, "I should explain to Bryony that it is good discipline to act in a dignified manner at all times."

"He shall explain it to me when we are driving, Mama," Bryony said firmly. "Come, Lucas."

"At once, my dear," he assented readily. With an apologetic glance at Lady Honoria, he added, "Pray you'll excuse us, Cousin?"

She shrugged, saying pettishly, "Of course, what other choice have I? It seems we are all bound to do my daughter's bidding. I hope you will enjoy your drive."

"How might it be otherwise?" he asked.

"Come." Bryony's tone was impatient. "I want to see your chestnuts." She darted from the room.

As Mr. Bardine walked slowly after her, Lady Honoria frowned. She was sure that she had read more than a mere cousinly affection in his eyes. Yet watching him lumber from the room, she grew more sanguine. It was obvious that her daughter felt no more than a warm friendship for this huge, clumsy youth. Indeed, she could almost feel sorry for him, for all she did not want Bryony allied with such a colossus. She frowned a second time. Actually, many dowagers of her acquaintance would have counted him an excellent match. He had a sizable fortune, a large acreage, and a beautiful home to grace it; and when Sir Bertram died, he would inherit the Baronetcy and even more property, including the Eaves.

Sir Bertram's mansion was a fine example of Tudor architecture, though not nearly as comfortable as that other family seat, Bardine Court. Lucas, with his exquisite taste and his love for antiquities, had filled the house with some rare treasures. Sir Anthony had acted as his advisor in some of these purchases, but he had told her that Lucas was even more discerning than himself when it came to the buying of tapestries, ivories and porcelains. All the same, Bryony could do much better. With her beauty and her own fortune, she could easily capture a Viscount or even an Earl.

There were few things that Lucas's expanding girth permitted him to do—he could not walk without becoming sadly breathless; he rarely rode, for even the sturdiest steed found it hard going to bear his weight for long. But, he did handle the ribbons well, and even Lady Honoria agreed that he had a way with horses. Bryony, watching him tool his curricle expertly through the crowded streets, smiled with pleasure. "They are beautiful animals," she commented, admiring the small heads and graceful bodies of the new chestnuts. "I think I do prefer them to the greys. Oh, it is delightful to be away from Mama . . . I find her a dead bore. I wish Papa might have lived. He shouldn't have always insisted upon my being so stiff and proper even when I am with you."

Mr. Bardine said commiseratingly, "Must be tedious. Imagine she doesn't want you to make an error when you're in the company of those who count."

"But you count, Lucas," she assured him earnestly. "I am so very glad you have come back. I have missed you frightfully."

"Have you, Bree?"

She nodded. "It has been so deadly dull, all the gentlemen pursuing me and saying such ridiculous things. You are never ridiculous."

"Am I not?" he demanded, his eyes twinkling. "That *is* a compliment."

"I have never found you so, Lucas, I do feel so comfortable with you. It's tiresome always being with people who insist on making love to one."

"Expect it must be," he agreed, edging past a flock of sheep. "Hope you are enjoying yourself a little."

"Oh, I expect I am," she allowed. "I like to dance. I prefer the waltz though Mama thinks it is not quite the thing. But that is a very old-fashioned point of view because it is being accepted everywhere. It is extremely exhilarating. Stephen waltzes beautifully and—oh, do be

18

careful, Lucas, you almost grazed the wheel of that coach!"

It was a cry that was echoed by Joseph, the diminutive groom who sat in the rear of the vehicle: "Cooo-er, nearly burned 'em, you did, sir."

"It was a near thing," Mr Bardine panted, reining in his horses and allowing the coach to pass him, the entire while mouthing apologies to its startled driver and its elderly passenger, a wizened gentleman, who stuck head and stick out of the window, shaking both, as he screamed about "great boobies" who were "not only ham-handed but bacon-brained and ought not to be allowed the freedom of the streets!"

Bryony, dissolving into laughter, darted a mischievous glance at her cousin, only to find him looking unexpectedly sober. "Come," she cried gaily, "I pray you did not take his rudeness to heart!"

"Eh?" He looked at her blankly.

"You frightened him."

"Whom?"

"The man in the coach, naturally. You must have been wool-gathering, Lucas."

"Um," Mr. Bardine grunted. "He come calling often? Stephen, I mean?"

"A few times." Bryony smiled. "Mama should count herself much in your debt. She has taken a great fancy to him. She quite agrees with you that he was most cruelly treated."

"And you . . . have you also taken a fancy to him, Bree?" He stared at her intently.

"He is well enough," she shrugged. Her eyes grew bright with laughter. "Chrissie Lawton thinks he is very romantic and I expect Mama does, too."

"Romantic?" he repeated with a slight frown.

Bryony nodded. "Chrissie loaned me a novel, which,

she told me, could have been about Stephen. I read it and it was, at least in some respects. Only think, Lucas, it concerned this handsome young man—his name was Algernon Trevalyan and he was raised in abject poverty like poor Stephen. Then he did a good deed and came to the attention of his cruel grandfather—though I have never thought of Great-Grandfather as particularly cruel, and Mama has said that Great-Uncle Orville was very wild and did a great many other things before he was cast off—but, anyway, Algernon's grandfather had cast off his daughter for marrying an impoverished clergyman. Eventually Algernon was restored to the bosom of his family and stood to inherit a great fortune as well as a dukedom, which meant he could wed Etherea Cummingford, his true love, whose father, a general, had never approved of poor Algernon. There was, of course, a great deal more to it. It ran to three volumes. It was entitled *The Lost Heir, or: Virtue Rewarded*. Of course, Stephen did not do a good deed, and he came to your attention rather than that of Great-Grandfather Bertram's and it was his father who married beneath him—so sad about his mother. I expect I ought to call her Great-Aunt Sophia or I should had she not succumbed of a broken heart after Great-Uncle Orville was killed in that coaching accident. Algernon's parents both died young, also. The author killed them off in the first volume. Algernon had a very hard time of it after that. I expect Stephen had, too."

"Expect so," Mr Bardine nodded.

"I think that play-actresses must be very much in demand. Chrissie has told me that many gentlemen have them, but that they usually do not marry them."

"Surely your Mama would not approve this discussion," he frowned.

"Of course not," Bryony agreed, "but she is not here to listen. Why do you expect Great-Uncle Orville found it necessary to wed his play-actress? Her whole name was Sophia Platt, was it not? That sounds very undistinguished. I imagine she must have been beautiful, though."

"Probably," Mr. Bardine said.

"I have a notion that Great-Uncle must have done something else besides merely marrying Miss Platt, otherwise I am sure Great-Grandfather would have forgiven him. After all, if Lady Harriet Wentworth could marry a footman . . . and which peer was it wed a butcher's daughter? Chrissie told me but I have forgotten."

"Not necessary to remember," he said.

"Lucas, do not be stuffy," she pleaded. "If I cannot speak frankly with you . . . oh, look!" she cried indignantly. "That horrid man . . . that poor beast is but skin and bones! Someone must stop him."

She pointed a trembling finger at a carter, who, having halted a wagon filled with large wooden barrels by the side of the road, was wielding his long leather whip over the quivering back of a lean and spavined horse. Unthinkingly, she was about to leap from the curricle when Mr. Bardine caught her arm and brought the vehicle to a jolting stop.

"Heads, Joseph," he called.

Tumbling from his perch, the groom ran forward to seize the bridles of the chestnuts while Mr. Bardine, handing the reins to Bryony, said, "Hold them tightly." He alighted with a speed amazing in one of his weight and stepped to the wagon; wrenching the whip from the fingers of the astonished carter, he broke it in two pieces and flung them down.

" 'Ere," yelled the man, blinking up at him belligerently. "Wot're ye about?"

His shrill whine was echoed by a butcher's assistant and several other assorted apprentices who had halted to watch the altercation. "Don't let yon fatty get the best o' ye!" jeered a reedy lad in a tanner's apron.

"Stow yer gab," screamed little Joseph, only to net another round of jeers and ribald comments on Mr. Bardine's size and shape, though it was also to be noted that not one of the crowd made any effort to come to the carter's assistance.

Mr. Bardine, however, appeared oblivious to the hecklers. Addressing himself to the carter, he asked, "How much will you take for that animal?"

" 'E's not for sale . . ." the carter began, then as Mr. Bardine moved nearer to the wagon, he huddled down in his seat saying defensively, "A guinea, me lud. 'E's me liveli'ood."

"Don't ye give'm near so much," shrilled Joseph, "for a nag wot's dead on 'er feet."

"Nah," yelled the onlookers, suddenly shifting loyalties, "Don't ye do it."

Producing a purse, Mr. Bardine extracted a coin. "Here's your money." Turning away from the carter, he called, "Joseph, unharness the mare and lead her to my stables—see that she receives prompt attention."

" 'Ere, wot am I to do wi' me wagon?" whined the carter.

"Try pullin' it yerself," screamed an apprentice. "Looks as if you was stronger'n that there 'orse."

Moving back to his curricle, Mr. Bardine climbed up, took the reins from Bryony, and called, "Get out of the way, Joseph."

As the little groom obeyed him, the horses plunged forward and they were off amidst ringing cheers from the fickle crowd.

"Lucas!" Bryony said breathlessly, "you broke the whip in half!"

"My lamentable temper," he apologized. "Never could bear to see animals mistreated. Should've liked to break it over his head . . . but lady present."

"Oh, you should not have taken that into account," she cried. "I should have loved to see you break it over his head. Why, I could hardly believe my eyes. I never imagined that you, of all people, would have enough courage to do such a thing."

He stared down at her for a long moment: "No?" he asked finally.

"No," she echoed, "I never, never did. Why you were actually heroic, Lucas. I vow, I cannot wait to tell Mama! She will not credit it, either. She is forever saying that you . . ." As she met his eyes, her words died on her tongue and it seemed to her as though the flush that warmed her cheeks extended all the way down to her toes. "I . . . I mean," she stuttered. "Well, it is just that I have never seen you so angry. You always appear so good-natured even . . . when you might think you . . . wouldn't be."

He nodded. "Expect I give that impression."

She was aware of a heavy pulse beating in her throat, "Lucas, I feel that without meaning to . . . I have hurt you. I never . . . it was only that . . . I was surprised. I mean not surprised but . . ."

"Hurt me?" he interrupted in a soothing voice. "No such thing, my dear."

Staring up into his eyes, she found their expression unreadable but, for some reason his easy dismissal had failed to convince her. "I hope I . . . did not. I mean that I was very proud of you . . . that is all I meant," she said earnestly.

"Kind of you to tell me," he smiled. "But it was nothing." He suddenly looked grim. "Ought to be a law against maltreating those poor beasts."

"Yes, there certainly ought to be," she agreed, relieved that he had changed the subject. It was, she decided, quite possible that he had not noticed her inadvertent admission regarding his bravery or lack of it. Equally unfortunate had been her reference to Lady Honoria's opinion of him, and her admission that she might agree with it—which she most certainly did not! It was only, she told herself, that she had never expected anything in the way of swift action from him nor had she believed that there could be so much strength in his soft white hands. She longed to better explain what she meant for her own satisfaction, but possibly that would only make matters worse. They had reached the end of the street and directly ahead of them was Hyde Park. She had expected that he would skirt it, for he had mentioned driving as far as Chelsea. Instead, he turned into it. "Oh," she said disappointedly, "I thought we were going further."

He shook his head. "It had best be the Park this morning, my dear. Recollect I've something I must see to."

"Oh," Bryony sighed, "I was hoping that we might have more time together. I . . ." She paused, wondering if, after all, she had wounded him or even angered him. It was very odd. Until that morning, she had believed him to be impervious to both emotions. She swallowed a large lump in her throat, wishing that she might call back those heedless remarks of a few moments ago. It would be terrible if she had alienated Lucas, whom she adored above all other people in the world. She was suddenly conscious of a great emptiness about her, almost as if,

24

at that moment, she were totally alone. With a little frightened cry, she turned toward Lucas, seizing his arm. "My dear. . ." she murmured and then was startled into silence as the chestnuts plunged ahead, only to be pulled in quickly by Mr. Bardine.

"Careful, Bryony," he said. "My driving arm. Is anything the matter?"

"No . . . nothing. How beautiful and green the park looks."

"Yes, it is at its best now," he agreed. "Shall we drive around the Serpentine?"

"I should like that," she said. "Lucas, when you were at the Court . . . did you go to the 'castle'? I do miss it . . . all our picnics there . . . we did have such lovely times."

Mr. Bardine did not answer. He appeared to be solely interested in negotiating a difficult turn. Finally he said, "It is well there is little traffic at this hour . . . I will need to take you back soon."

"Will you? Why?" Her sense of fear had returned.

"Business I have neglected, my dear."

"Should you like to leave immediately?" she asked. "I would not mind."

"Would you not?" he demanded.

"No," she assured him.

"After all," Mr. Bardine smiled, "I expect there are many who will take you driving in the Park, are there not?"

"Oh, yes, many," she agreed brightly. "Am I not an Incomparable?"

He nodded. "I have always thought so." He wheeled his horses about. "I hope that I may avail myself of my cousinly privilege and take you driving later in the week?"

"Of course you may," she said. "I would rather be with you than anyone—I really would, Lucas."

He smiled. "I am indeed honored, my dear."

She expelled a sigh of relief. She had been, she decided, over-anxious, imbuing Lucas with a sensibility that was quite foreign to his happily uncomplicated nature. She was glad of that. She had not relished that alien sense of desolation and regret that had briefly invaded her consciousness. If she were to be happy, she realized, Lucas must remain Lucas as she had always known him— her very best friend.

TWO

It was less than three-quarters of an hour after they had begun their drive that Mr. Bardine escorted his second cousin toward the door of her house. Bryony, looking up at his large perspiring face, was moved to say, "It is, perhaps, well that we have returned earlier. You seem very warm, Lucas."

"Am a bit," he agreed.

"You had better rest once you have returned to your lodgings."

"Shall. Kind of you to be concerned."

"But I always am," she assured him earnestly.

"Very kind, my dear."

"Do stop saying that I am kind," Bryony entreated, only to receive a look of blank surprise from Mr. Bardine. She bit back a sigh. The lump had returned to her throat; for surely Lucas was behaving with a politeness that teetered perilously upon the brink of that bland formality with which mere acquaintances were wont to address each other! If he had not seized upon that moment to ring the bell, she would have tried to question him about the sense of estrangement she was experiencing, in the hope of mending matters between them—if, indeed, she told herself, she were not refining too much upon it; perhaps there was no need for mending. But then, a footman opened the door and Mr. Bardine ceremoniously bowed her inside.

"You will want to come and bid farewell to Mama." She gestured at the twin portals opening on the drawing room.

"I rather think, my dear—" he began, only to be interrupted as Bryony continued: "And you will go with us to the Opera tonight, will you not?"

"The Opera?"

"Yes, they are performing *Artaserse* by Cimarosa, and Stephen has convinced Mama that she must see it. Imagine, she has actually consented to come, much as she is always telling me she cannot abide Italian music!"

"My cousin is very persuasive," murmured Mr. Bardine.

"He most certainly is," Bryony agreed. "Will you come, Lucas?"

"I should be delighted . . . if room can be found for me," Mr. Bardine replied.

"I am sure there will be room. Chrissie will be there, but I do not think Stephen has invited anyone else. Mama will know. Come." Impulsively, she pulled open one of the doors only to pause on the threshold as a melliflous voice issued through the aperture, reciting a poem by Lord Byron.

> When we two parted,
>   In silence and tears,
> Half broken-hearted,
>   To sever for years . . .

"Oh," Bryony hissed to Mr. Bardine, who had stepped hastily to her side. "It's Stephen!"

"So it would seem." Mr. Bardine, reaching around her, pulled the door open, revealing Lady Honoria still reclining on her sofa, while, at her side, a young man with a book in his hand looked up startled and jumped to his feet.

"Cousin Bryony!" he cried. "And Lucas! Well met, very well met!" As he came toward them, the contrast between the two cousins was almost ludicrous; for, where Lucas Bardine was ponderous and clumsy, Stephen Bardine was slender, and grace itself. There was no doubt that the mode of dress promulgated by Beau Brummell was exceedingly becoming to him. He was blessed with a well-proportioned figure, and the close-fitting checked jacket with its nipped-in waist and the tight black trousers set off his wide shoulders and narrow hips, while his cravat, tied in that style called the "Oriental," was a frame for a strong cleft chin. Any resemblance between the two men was evident only in their coloring: both had thick dark hair and brown eyes, though these, in Stephen's case, were well-opened and only one more handsome feature in an extremely engaging countenance.

"Well met!" he cried a third time. "I was desolated when I learned I had missed you, Cousin Bryony . . . and Lucas, I heard yesterday that you were back from

Brighton. I must say I was surprised, but Cousin Honoria tells me that you are a sufferer from a *mal de mer* that extends even to the beaches!"

Bryony gave Stephen a sharp glance, wondering if he was daring to make sport of the man through whose good offices he had been rescued from obscurity. Though she read only concern in his limpid gaze, she made haste to say, "Poor Lucas had a narrow escape from drowning as a child."

"So Cousin Honoria has explained," Stephen said. "It is a great pity. I myself am extremely partial to the sea—but be that as it may, it is pleasant to have you once more in London, Cousin Lucas."

"Most kind of you to say so," murmured Mr. Bardine. "Am glad to have met you here. Was coming to look for you directly upon leaving. Wouldn't have found you."

"To look for me?" Stephen's brown eyes narrowed. "Is there something of import you'd confide?"

"A trifling matter," Mr. Bardine said. "Perhaps you will come out with me now . . . will explain it to you."

"Oh," Lady Honoria protested, "you are not going to take Stephen away? He was reading me some of Lord Byron's poems." She smiled at Stephen. "Most eloquently, too."

"You are too kind." Stephen bowed. "The eloquence is in the writing."

"I beg to differ with you, dear Stephen." The glance Lady Honoria threw at him could almost be classified as languishing. "The writing is elegant, but the eloquence stems solely from your lips."

"Mama!" Bryony was suddenly eager to end what she could consider only as an embarrassingly fatuous display on her mother's part. "If Lucas deems it important to speak with Stephen, I think we must relinquish his presence. After all, we shall meet at the Opera tonight and . . . I hope Lucas may join us there. Is that possible, Stephen?" Seemingly unconscious of her parent's glare, and silently congratulating herself upon having covered so many important points in so brief a time, she bestowed a beguiling smile upon her cousin.

"By all means," Stephen replied. "We should be delighted to have you, Lucas. I hope you will come."

"Shall, if it meets with your approval as well, Cousin Honoria." Mr. Bardine said.

"Of course. Why should it not?" Lady Honoria said. "Besides, the party is entirely of Stephen's devising."

"There," Bryony said triumphantly, "what did I tell you, Lucas?"

"In that case, should be happy to attend," he said. He moved toward the door and, with an inquiring glance at Stephen, added, "Must be on my way."

"And I will come with you, of course." Smiling at Lady Honoria, Stephen handed the small volume of poems to her. "I hope that you will enjoy these, Cousin."

"But you cannot give them to me," she protested. "Not when the poet himself has inscribed the flyleaf to you."

"He has inscribed another for me. We are good friends," he assured her, "and Byron is always eager that his work find a haven in the homes of the discerning and the appreciative."

"I do thank you." Lady Honoria actually flushed with pleasure. "But I hope that you will soon come to read more of them to me."

"Of course, I shall." He kissed her hand. Then with an ingratiating smile that embraced both ladies, he bowed.

"I bid you good morning, Cousins." Shooting an impish glance at Mr. Bardine, he said, "Lead on, Macduff!"

"Quite so," Lucas Bardine returned. "Your servant, ladies," he added with one of his small bows.

As the doors closed behind the two gentlemen, Lady Honoria said crossly, "You returned uncommonly early, Bryony."

"I expect that was because Lucas wanted to find Stephen, who was here, I might add, uncommonly early," Bryony retorted.

Her implication was lost on her mother, who said, "Yes, he had mentioned those poems yesterday and since I had expressed a desire to see them, he came to show them to me. He is the most thoughtful young man. It is the greatest pity . . ." She paused, shaking her head.

"What is, Mama?"

"I expect you'll not agree with me," Lady Honoria said tartly, "but I am of the opinion that Stephen Bardine is far better suited to be Grandfather's heir than that great clod of—'

"Mama," Bryony interrupted, fixing her with a furious eye, "I beg that you will say no more! There can be no comparison between them. Indeed, I do not even like Stephen!" She had spoken with more defiance than truth, but even as the words left her lips, she realized with a slight shock that, after all, she meant what she said.

"You do not like him?" Lady Honoria snapped. "Might I know why?"

"I . . . I do not trust him," Bryony said thoughtfully.

"I think you must be mad!" her mother exclaimed.

Frowning, Bryony shook her head. "No—" She quite longed to state that it was Lady Honoria who was sadly deluded if not madly infatuated. However, since such frank speech could certainly never be tolerated from a daughter to her mother, she contented herself by saying pacifically, "I fear I am a bit out of sorts, Mama. I think I must rest before luncheon, if you would excuse me."

"By all means," Lady Honoria assented. "I am not surprised that you are out of temper; you were up very late." Pointedly, she added, "Stephen told me that you created a sensation at the ball last night."

"That was kind of him," Bryony said. As she left the room she saw her mother gently patting the volume her cousin had given her, a far-away smile on her lips. With a little *moue* of distaste, Bryony hurried out. She wished that she might discuss this problem with Lucas. Then she frowned and tears started to her eyes; for it seemed to her that the gap between them had perceptibly widened even in the few minutes that had passed since he had accompanied her into the drawing room. Usually, when he left her, there was always some special little look or nod, but today there had been nothing. It struck her that it might be very difficult to have such a discussion with him. It might even be impossible.

Coming into her chamber, she found that her maid, Mary, had arranged the bouquet of spring flowers Mr. Lucas Bardine had sent her in a crystal vase beside her bed. Touching them, and seeing among them the narcissus which he knew to be her favorite, she sank down among her pillows and began to cry.

Mr. Lucas Bardine occupied lodgings on Portman Street; and it was to these that he bore his cousin Stephen, immediately upon quitting the De Beaufre establishment. He had been singularly noncommittal during the drive and consequently, once the two men were alone in his small but exquisitely furnished parlor, Stephen said with some urgency, "What might this trifling matter be, Cousin."

Looking at him with a severity quite foreign to his usually benign gaze, Mr. Bardine said accusingly, "It appears to me that you have misrepresented certain facts of your life, Stephen."

Stephen's eyes widened. "Misrepresented," he said. "But when I came to you, I told you of my poverty and my work as an actor, even in such miserable spots as Bartholomew Fair, when I was endeavoring to support my poor mother—"

"Your poor mother, whom you represented as deceased," Mr Bardine interrupted sternly.

"Which she is and has been these three years past —of consumption brought on by starvation," Stephen Bardine said bitterly, his eyes straying past a small gilt and crystal clock to a marvelously carved jade goddess. There were similar *objets d'art* on tables and shelves throughout the room and his expression grew censorious, as if he were contrasting his cousin's comfortable existence with his own earlier struggles.

Generally, Mr. Bardine was highly sensitive to such nuances, and on other occasions he had been more than a little apologetic. At this present moment, however, his manner underwent no change. Fixing a cold eye upon Stephen, he commented, "It is not often that the deceased can write letters."

"L—Letters?" Stephen faltered. "W—What can you mean?"

Reaching inside his coat, Mr. Bardine extracted a small piece of notepaper, much creased and stained. "I mean this." Without handing it to Stephen, he read,

" 'Dear Mr. Lucas Bardine:

If I wasn't in sore trouble, I would not never pen this letter, but my boy Stephen, who has promised to give me monies hasn't never let me have so much as a groat and I am starving. Help me. I beg of you.'

"It is signed Sophia Bardine and it gives an address in Covent Garden."

Stephen had gone alarmingly pale. He essayed a shaky and unconvincing laugh. "It . . . it is a forgery."

"Is it?" Mr. Bardine fixed probing eyes upon his cousin's face.

Stephen's own gaze flickered. "Y—Yes, she . . . she's dead. It is as I told you . . . she is dead these three years and more. The letter was written by someone who knows of my good fortune . . . someone from the old days, who is envious and wishes me ill . . . I assure you."

"Then why are you so frightened, Stephen?"

"I . . . am not frightened, I am *furious*," Stephen stated. "You do believe me?" He drew a deep breath. "You must. I swear to you, Cousin, my mother is dead. Surely you cannot think I would neglect her. Were she living, she would be with me. Mama was all the world to me."

"I see. . . ." Mr. Bardine continued to regard him closely. "You think this might be a way to extort money from me?"

"I most certainly do!" Stephen assured him earnestly. Then looking down, he added, "You . . . uh . . . you've not told anyone about receiving this letter, have you? Not Miss de Beaufre or . . . her mother?"

Mr. Bardine shook his head. "Wouldn't mention it to anyone until I'd discussed it with you."

Stephen drew another deep, tremulous breath. "I am

glad of that. There's no need to . . . to trouble her or Cousin Honoria with so . . . flagrant a lie. I pray you will let me have that paper. I believe I know its source and I will deal with the man who sent it."

"The man?" Mr. Bardine inquired.

"I . . . I am sure I know his identity. He was one who used to do odd jobs for us in return for sharing our poor lodgings. He slept on the floor in the cellar. He was an out-and-out villain, a pimp, but he was useful at the last . . . for sometimes he worked for an apothecary and was able to . . . bring her medicines I could not afford." He raised a haggard face to Mr. Bardine. "You do believe me, do you not?"

There was a silence during which Stephen moved restlessly in his chair, wringing his hands together, his eyes darting about the room, seeming to look everywhere but at his cousin's face. Finally, Mr. Bardine said heavily, "Should not like to think you'd betray me, Stephen."

"Betray you?"

"Should have said, betray the trust I've put in you," Mr. Bardine amended.

"How might I convince you?" Stephen sighed. He rose suddenly. "I know how!" he said purposefully: "I shall seek out the man whom I know must have sent it . . . and he will tell you the truth of it."

"How can you be sure of finding him?" Mr. Bardine asked.

"I will find him. Meanwhile, I pray you will trust me, Cousin."

Stephen looked piteously at him. "I swear to you that . . . that this must be the way of it." Snatching the paper from Mr. Bardine's grasp, he crumpled it savagely and threw it on the floor. "And in my mother's name! I shall make him rue the day that he ever resorted

36

to such measures. You'll not be troubled again, I promise you." Whirling, Stephen strode from the room.

Mr. Bardine shook his head and sighed deeply. He picked up the crumpled paper and thoughtfully smoothed it out. As he stared at it, a puckered frown creased his forehead; then, nodding, he rang for his valet.

"Rudd," he said as the man entered, "I want you to get me a hackney."

The valet looked at him in astonishment. "A . . . a hackney, sir?"

"At once," Mr. Bardine said resolutely.

The stairs were narrow and broken, and the slatternly woman, who held the candle that was lighting Mr. Bardine up them, looked back at him with a sneer written large upon her thin, unprepossessing features. "Ye think ye can make it?" she demanded mockingly.

Mr. Bardine, his handkerchief pressed against his nostrils to shut out the noxious odors emanating from the gin shop directly below, panted in acquiescence. "How much further it is, my good woman?" he asked faintly.

"My good woman!" Her shrill laughter grated on his ears. "I ought to throw ye a kiss for that, I'm thinkin'. Only maybe you'd not like me kisses, eh? Ain't often we get a cove like yerself in this dossing-ken. 'Er ladyship'll be mighty pleased to see you. . . . Ain't much further, up two more steps'n down this 'ere passage. Door at the end."

Joining her at the top of the stairs, Mr. Bardine was forced by necessity to stand against the wall, gasping for air. Looking down the dark, dank corridor, the shock and horror he had been experiencing, ever since entering the foul hole below, increased. Unlike many of the young sprigs of the nobility, Mr. Bardine, possibly because of his great bulk, did not possess an adventurous spirit; consequently he had never sought the excitement attendant upon a foray into the slums that lay cheek-by-jowl with the broad streets and magnificent mansions of the city. Though he had listened with some sympathy to Stephen Bardine's descriptions of his deprived childhood in just such an atmosphere, he had utterly failed to envision the filth of those narrow streets and the degradation of their inhabitants.

He shuddered, remembering the young girls who had solicited him before he had made his way into Mabe's gin shop, and shuddered again, thinking of its noisome interior. Half of its customers were sprawled on the floor in various stages of inebriation, while other members of the scarlet sisterhood of the streets—scrawny women with heavily rouged faces and dyed hair—hovered near them, exchanging rough jests or equally rough caresses with those still sober enough to talk, or stretching claw-like fingers beneath the jackets of those who had succumbed to too much of that liquor so appropriately nicknamed "Blue Ruin", their thievery totally ignored by the proprietor. His ears had been assailed by their derisive laughter as he had maneuvered his unwieldy body toward the plank that served as a bar and, striving to make his cultured tones heard above the babble of voices, had asked for Mrs. Sophia Bardine.

He had hoped devoutly that Stephen had been telling the truth and that his mother was, as he had insisted, dead. Unfortunately, Mr. Bardine's fears had been realized. He had been told that she resided in the lodging upstairs; and now, as he prepared for the fateful meeting, he could not help conjuring up a vision of her son, as he had so recently seen him, sitting in Lady Honoria's drawing room, reading poetry to her. His sense of outrage deepened—reading poetry, while his wretched mother lay in this enclave of thieves, harlots and drunkards!

"Caught yer breath, dearie?" inquired his guide.

"Yes."

"Then c'mon along but mind ye watch yer step. There's places where the flooring's gone rotten; best stick close to the wall."

"Thank you," he said, moving against it and grimacing as he felt what he guessed to be a century's worth of dust and dirt beneath his fingertips. He could, he thought ironically, well understand his cousin's imperfectly concealed fear of his finding his mother in such cirumstances. His guilt had been apparent in every word he had uttered. Evidently, shock at his mother's desperate action had robbed him of his usual *sang-froid*. Certainly, he had been far different than the self-possessed young man who had sought Mr. Bardine out at his lodgings all those months ago. He shook his head sadly, annoyed with himself for his gullibility—but Stephen's story had seemed so plausible—and there was no denying the relationship. He bore a distinct resemblance to a portrait of his father hanging in the gallery at the Eaves. Probably he had been ashamed of his mother, and quite possibly he had plenty of reason for that. Bits of family gossip concerning the disastrous marriage had convinced Mr. Bardine that his uncle was not the first of the woman's protectors. Furthermore, there was talk that she had encouraged her husband to steal a large sum from Sir Bertram in order to pay for jewels and other finery. However, Mr. Bardine reflected, if Stephen had come to him and stated the case honestly, he would have helped care for the poor creature. As it was he could only bitterly regret his wholehearted acceptance of Stephen's tale, and worse than that, his haste in introducing him into

London society—and worst of all, to Lady Honoria and Bryony.

Thinking of Bryony, he winced. He had trusted her, too, believing in some deep recess of his mind that she loved him, if not passionately at least with a deep affection that saw beyond his obese body and into his soul. He had believed that until this morning, when a few hasty words had convinced him that, in common with most of his acquaintances, she thought him a weak, ungainly figure of fun. He recalled, too, her earnest—and, to his mind, inept—attempts to banish this supposition, and knew it would be up to him to pretend that he had forgotten the revelations of that moment. But he could never forget it nor, he knew with a mixture of anger and regret, would he ever forgive it. There was a hollow feeling in his chest as he arrived at this conclusion, for he had loved her as he had loved no one else in his twenty-four years of life.

"'Ere," said the woman, "don't ye go no further."

Startled, he realized that in his preoccupation he had walked almost to the end of the corridor, and under the flickering light of the candle, to his horror he saw that a large rat had poked its bewhiskered snout from a hole in the wainscoting, scurrying back when the woman tapped on the door facing them. There was no response. "Maybe she's sleeping," he ventured.

"We'll see." She produced a key, unlocked the door, and thrust it back so that it banged against the wall. "Sophie, dearie," she called. "Got a visitor for ye."

There was a feeble moan from inside, "Be ye funnin' me, Clara?"

"Nah, 'e's a fine gentleman, a real swell wot wants to see ye."

"A gentleman . . ." the voice inside repeated unbelieving; "I sent a letter to a gentleman . . . a Mr. Lucas Bardine, wot did so well by my son . . . him wot thinks 'e's too good for 'is poor ma. But I didn't 'ear nothin' back."

Mr. Bardine said loudly, "Mrs. Sophia Bardine?"

"Yes . . . be you 'im?" the woman inside asked with a note of excitement in her faltering tones. "Oh, would ye come in? I'm that sick I cannot rise from me bed."

"G'arn." The woman named Clara sketched a curtsey. "The lady awaits ye."

He moved into a darkened room. In the far corner he saw a narrow bed and on it, a figure huddled under a ragged cover. As he started toward it, he was aware of the door creaking shut behind him and, shockingly, the sound of a key in the lock. He stopped immediately and in that moment someone sprang from the shadows behind him. He felt an arm go around his throat. With a heave of his shoulders, he shook off his assailant and turned to do battle; but even as he did, something struck him on he head and vivid splashes of brightness flickered in his eyes for a moment before weakness and pain overcame him and he toppled to the floor.

"Are you quite sure he's unconscious, Uncle Oliver?"

"Bless you boy, 'is 'ead ain't that 'ard."

The words swam into Mr. Bardine's consciousness on a wave of agony. His head was hurting dreadfully. Still he had the presence of mind to stifle a groan as the conversation continued in the darkness around him.

"Did I not tell you that letter would fetch him?" It was Stephen speaking.

"Aye, aye, sir, you did . . . though I'm damned if I know 'ow you could've been so sure about it."

"Because I understand him. He has a soft heart and a weak brain beneath all that blubber. He is a mass of sentiment, is my dear Cousin Lucas. I have known him to weep over a sad song, so how could a mother's plight fail to move him?"

"Be that as it may, boy, I'm blowed if I know wot we can do wi' 'im, 'cept feed 'im to the fishes."

"No," Stephen protested, "not murder."

"It'll be murder one way or t'other . . . Lord love you, look at 'im!"

A small lighted candle was thrust toward Mr. Bardine's face so suddenly that he had not the time to close his eyes.

"Cor, 'e's awake."

In the glow from that all-too-revealing flame, Mr. Bardine glimpsed his Cousin Stephen's gloating eyes and the rugged face of the man with him. Then he saw the cudgel descending. He tried to move his head out of the way but to no avail. He knew another moment of blinding agony and then, mercifully, a curtain of darkness blotted out everything.

The man called Oliver grabbed a handful of Mr. Bardine's hair and lifting his head from the floor, he then let it fall. There was no respose from his victim. " 'E's truly gone this time . . . 'e 'eard us . . . maybe we ought to kill 'im," he said.

"No." Stephen smiled down at his cousin's recumbent form. "He did me a good turn and I'll do him another. Let him live until he dies of—natural causes." His tone was grim. "Let him know what it means to be beaten and starved . . . to work your fingers to the bone the way I did when I was a child, while he was growing fat on his fine estates. Let him sweat and suffer a little before he dies." He laughed. "The cream of the jest, my dear Uncle, is that he is terrified of the sea."

"Terrified, is he?" A laugh rumbled out of his uncle. " 'E won't last long aboard the *Eagle* . . . if the mate don't kill 'im, the men will an' if they don't do 'im in, the grub will, 'n if that don't do it—'e'll get 'is once they see action an' accordin' to my friend Mr. Briggs, it won't be no time at all afore we're shootin' it out wit' the Yankees . . ."

"You do not imagine he'll be able to convince the Captain of his, er, position?"

"Nah, 'ow many times do I 'ave to tell ye that the Captain don't listen to wot comes aboard through the press gangs, an' if 'e was to listen, wouldn't be to a bloke wot's in a seaman's jersey an 'oo's got a bloody big anchor tattooed on 'is upper arm an' a square-rigger 'crost 'is chest. An expanse like that brings out me artistry, me lad. I'll give 'im a couple o' beauties an' they'll be wrote down in the Muster Book along wi' 'is description'n so if 'e gets smart'n tries to jump ship, 'e'll be 'anged the quicker. Any way you look at it, me lad, 'e'll be in Davy Jones's locker afore long an' ye'll be eatin' off 'is gold plate 'n swillin' 'is liquor 'n thinkin' good thoughts about yer old uncle, eh, Sir Stephen?"

"This Briggs . . . you're sure he will be sailing on the *Eagle?*"

"Sure as I'm standin' 'ere, an' 'e'll let me know when and 'ow." He laughed. "Only 'tis a rare shame you're no longer on the boards, my boy."

"Why is that?" Stephen demanded.

"Yer did a masterly job o' bein' yer ma. I swear if it didn't sound like old Soph 'erself afore the 'Blue Ruin' done 'er in."

Stephen laughed grimly. "I prefer this role. It's for a longer run and the pay is guaranteed, my dear Uncle."

The overture to *Artaserses* was at an end and in the brightly lighted reaches of the theater known as Covent Garden, those members of the audience who were not ogling the courtesans who strolled up and down the aisles or preened themselves in their boxes, or were not quarreling among themselves in the balconies, or having confidential conversations in the pit about the outcome of the latest cockfight or the Prime Miniser's folly in his handling of the American question, clapped politely.

In the front of a box almost directly over the stage sat Lady Honoria, looking exceptionally well in a gown of pink satin that added a glow to her pale skin. A turban of the same material covered her head and she had chosen to wear the De Beaufre diamonds, a necklace that had been in the family since the days of Queen Anne. Though the jewels were in an old-fashioned setting, she could not bear to have them reset since, as her husband's first bride-gift to her, they had a sentimental value that, in her estimation, must supercede the exigencies of fashion.

Next to her sat Miss Christine Lawton, Bryony's best female friend. She was small, dark and vivacious; and though Lady Honoria had been a little worried that their guest's mulberry-colored ensemble would war with her own pink, it actually managed to blend in very nicely. It was a becoming shade for the girl, complementing her olive complexion and clinging to a figure which, while small, was most shapely. However, while Miss Lawton was considered quite attractive, the gentlemen whose quizzing-glasses were trained on that box were in accord that its third feminine occupant put the other pair in the shade. Miss Bryony de Beaufre's curls were dressed *à la*

Grecque and ornamented with a small diamond crescent. She wore a single strand of pearls around her lovely neck and her simple white satin gown put one Marquis audibly in mind of a "goddess newly descended from Olympus." His friend, though less inclined toward classical allusions, agreed that she was ravishingly beautiful.

Rather than acknowledging the beaux who vied for her attention, Miss de Beaufre's anxious eyes kept straying to the empty chair to the left of her cousin Stephen. He was looking his best in a black satin coat and ruffled evening shirt and he, too, was the recipient of many glances, envious on the part of the male contingent and languishing from the female. It was noted by some of the eagle-eyed dowagers in other boxes that Lady Honoria was in the habit of staring back at him almost as often as she scanned the auditorium or the stage. Bryony's attention, however, remained on that empty chair.

"I cannot imagine what has detained Lucas," she said for the third time in as many minutes.

"And I cannot imagine why it should concern you," hissed Miss Lawton. "Do give a smile to the Duke. He has been trying to capture your attention for the last quarter hour."

"Bother the Duke!" Bryony murmured.

"I should not worry." Stephen leaned forward. "When we parted this afternoon, he assured me he was much pleased at the prospect of the Opera. As you yourself remarked, Cousin Bryony, the streets are extremely cluttered tonight. If he did not start on time, he would have had some difficulty in forcing his way through them."

"And through the crowds in front of the theater," Miss Lawton declared with a slightly derisive smile. "Poor Lucas is constitutionally unable to hurry."

"Lucas is usually punctuality itself," Bryony began and then paused, her eyes lighting as the door to the box was pushed open. "Oh, this must be he!"

Stephen, confronted by the mental image of an inert, tarpaulin-shrouded bulk being heaved onto a river-barge, its chest and arm discolored and swollen—the results of his maternal uncle's efforts with a tattooing needle—thrust a trembling hand between his knees and stared at that widening portal with a horrified fascination, but the gentleman who appeared looked merely discomfited. "I . . . I beg your pardon," he whispered. "Wrong place . . . pardon." Bowing and flushing, he hastily backed out.

Stephen, glancing at Bryony, hoped that she had not noticed his alarm. A moment later his fears were allayed as she said half-tearfully, "I do not know what can be keeping him. I pray he has not met with an accident."

"Of course he has not," Christine Lawton averred.

"Shhhhh," Lady Honoria cautioned, gesturing toward the stage. "Grassini is singing."

Bryony's anxious gaze was on Stephen. "Do you know, I cannot help but feel that something has . . . happened to him." She sighed.

"Come." He gave her a cajoling smile. "You refine too much upon it. I have the notion that dear Cousin Lucas is quite indestructible."

THREE

The first rays of a feeble April sun stole through the dusty glass of a window facing one of the noisome alleys of Covent Garden. They illumined a battered armoire and a sagging old four-poster long divested of its curtains, and lingered on the much-mended comforter and dingy sheet that covered its two occupants. One of them, a lean, dark young man with a few threads of white in his heavy brown locks, blinked himself awake and lay quietly for a moment, letting his eyes rove over the cracked window, the dusty walls with their stained and peeling paper with its incongruous scattering of apple blossoms, and then to the ragged carpet stretching across the slanted floor.

Outside, the street ran higgledy-piggledy between buildings which looked as if they were in immediate danger of falling down, but they had looked that way four years ago. They had not changed and nor had the gin shop below. There was still the plank of a counter, still the drunks on the floor and the predatory whores waiting to rob and strip them. None of that had changed. Only he had changed—changed to the point where the filth of the streets and the dirt of the cheap lodging house was so much a fact of his present life that neither now had the power to disgust him. Indeed, the chamber he had occupied for the past two days was better than many in which he had awakened. At least it had a bed with a mattress, however old, lumpy and sagging. He sucked in a deep breath of air and expelled it, stretching out his arms and touching the headboard behind him. The slight smile that twisted his lips had an element of saturnine humor in it as he reminded himself that, in this chamber, he was not far from the room of his "birth." He sent his mind back those four years and heard the conversation that had taken place before the cudgel had dropped him to the floor. Every word of it had been fury-seared into his brain.

It was that conversation that had brought him back to this slum—even though he feared it might be a fool's errand. It was more than possible that the man he had heard addressed as "Uncle Oliver," and whose surname could be Platt since that was the maiden name of the actress Sophia, might not necessarily be an *habitué* of the gin shop. Yet he had had to come. He had promised himself he would if ever he survived the horrors into which he had been plunged on that fateful day. Well, he *had* survived; and yesterday he had discovered that a man named Oliver Platt had indeed been known to Mabe, the proprietor of the gin shop. Platt had been a sometime sailor who had operated a tattoo parlor not far from these lodgings, but was long gone, disappeared or dead. Little matter; the information Platt would have given him—willingly or otherwise—would have been useful, but not vital. If alive, he would be found and dealt with in time. If dead . . . he had merely anticipated his fate. The young man wondered who else might have died in the ensuing years. Though he had long ago decided that all such solicitations were futile, he found that he could still pray fervently to God or the Devil that Stephen Bardine remained among the living so that he might have the pleasure of revenge. He had evolved a partial plan as to the nature of that revenge. It was one that—consequences be damned—he would not leave to his grandfather and to the due process of law. Just as his cousin had been an active participant in his own removal, he yearned to return the favor and with more lasting success. He more than yearned—he brought a fist down on the bed—it had been the meat and drink that had kept him alive through four years of anguish and misery.

A sleepy murmur reached him, and the frown that had been etched deep into his sun-browned countenance was smoothed away as he looked at the girl, who, until that moment, had been slumbering at his side. In the morning light she appeared less fresh than she had when he had picked her up the previous night, but still she was prettier than many who had shared his bed. He would be surprised to learn that she was much over sixteen but her pink-and-white complexion suggested that the tale she had told him, of being abducted by one of the old crones who frequented the inns where coaches from the country halted, was probably true. Many of the drabs who strolled about the Garden had similar histories.

"Mornin', love," she said, looking at him out of drowsy blue eyes. "Give us a kiss, do."

Shaking his head, he sat up and briskly detached her clinging arms when she would have pulled him down beside her again. "I have to rise, child; I must be on my way soon."

"Why so soon?" She ran a practiced hand over his chest, tracing the pattern of a large square-rigger, complete with sails done in vivid red inks and sporting a female figurehead on its prow. "Where'll you ship this time, love?"

"Nowhere. My seafaring days are at an end."

"I don't believe it," she laughed, touching the big blue anchor tattooed on his upper arm. "You'll be off wi' the next tide." Then reaching for his other arm she contemplated a huge red V that marked his swelling biceps. "This seems like it's still slightly swollen," she remarked.

He grimaced. "I had it done the day before we dropped anchor in Portsmouth."

"You must've been foxed."

"I was," he said ruefully. "Foxed or mad."

"Wot's it stand for, the name of your sweetheart ... Virginia?" she asked curiously.

His gaze hardened. "It could stand for Virginia or Vanessa or Viola ... or Victory ... or Vengeance."

"Vengeance?" she repeated; and, seeing that his features had gone very grim, she uttered a little cry: "I wish you'd not look that way."

"What way?"

"Like you was ill-wishin' somebody. My Grannie useta tell me that curses come 'ome to roost."

"Do they?" He slipped from the bed. "Well, that is a hazard I must chance."

She looked admiringly at his body. Most of the sailors she had known were on the chunky side—but he was tall and moved with a sinuous grace and, though his chest was broad, it tapered to a slender waist and narrow hips. She had been a little wary of his heavily muscled arms, but he had not used them to squeeze the life out of her the way some of the men did. He had pleasured her as well as himself, which was unique; but he was unique in many ways. Then she shook her head, for as he moved toward the window, the sun showed her the scars that she had felt when she had lain with him the previous night. They were even worse than she had imagined. From shoulder to buttocks his back was seamed with the marks that only the cat-o'-nine-tails would leave. She frowned. She had seen other sailors scored in the same manner, but somehow she would not have expected him to have suffered the cruel punishment. He had sustained other injuries, too; there were scars on his legs and a deep depression on one thigh, which might have been left by a bullet.

"I thought you come in on a merchantman," she said.

"I did," he replied, "out of Provincetown."

"That'd be in America?"

"Yes."

"Was you in the wars then?"

He nodded. "I was on a ship called the *Eagle*. It went down in the Battle of New Orleans."

"Where's that?"

"In a state called Louisiana." Moving to a table on which was a basin and an ewer, he splashed out some water and after washing himself, he took a razor and a strip of mirror out of a small, shabby portmanteau and lathering his face, he began to shave.

She was silent until he had finished. "Wot's it like, Louisiana?"

51

"Hot and swampy."

"That don't tell me much," she complained.

"I didn't see much of it—save for its prison."

"You was in prison?" she gasped.

"Yes, with those of our crew who survived the sinking of the ship."

"Cooo-er, that must 'ave been 'ard," she said pityingly.

"No harder than the *Eagle*."

"Was you there long?"

"Until I was shot trying to escape. Then I was in a hospital."

"Was you hurt bad?"

"I didn't die from it." He shrugged. Moving to the armoire, he took out an armful of garments.

She looked at them with some admiration. "You look to 've done yourself well," she approved.

"They're good quality," he agreed, with one of his twisted smiles "It's to be hoped I'll not meet up with any of their former owners."

"Not likely," she giggled.

"No, I imagine not."

"Do not get dressed yet, love," she held out her arms. "You treated me nice last night . . . I'd like to return the favor."

He shook his head. "You're a good girl, Nance, but I've some traveling ahead of me and I've delayed long enough already." As he went on with his dressing, she watched admiringly. If his muslin shirt was a little stained on one sleeve and the buckskin pantaloons a trifle too big for him, his fawn-colored waistcoat fitted over them neatly, as did a dark blue coat with the long tails which were the very crack of fashion and had undoubtedly cost its first purchaser a pretty penny. She could see that his boots were a little cracked, but one would not look at them when confronted with his handsome face rising above a beautifully arranged cravat. Once he had clapped his tall beaver hat on his well-brushed hair, she looked at him in utter amazement.

"Cooo-er, if you ain't grand by 'alf," she breathed.

"Am I?"

To her surprise there was a trace of anxiety in his tone. "You could be one of them dandies wot sits in the bow window at Whites, you could," she marveled.

"Fine feathers," he laughed.

"It's more than that," she said positively, "it's the way you talk, too, like one o' them."

"But you and I know otherwise, do we not, sweet Nance?" His eyes darkened. "Without the proper apparel, and with such decorations or . . . lacerations as mark me, a man's no better than a wharf rat—and that's the truth of it."

"It's not," she disputed earnestly. "Even without your good duds, you're different. I been thinkin' ever since I met up wi' you last night that you wasn't like any other sailor I ever seen. You was different to begin with. . . . Where'll you be goin' now you're dressed so fine?"

"Shall we say, my dear, that I am off to seek my fortune?" he replied with a look that sent a chill through her.

"It ain't good," she whispered. "It aint."

"What isn't?" he demanded.

"'Atin' somebody the way you do. Like I said, they comes 'ome to roost, curses."

"And, as I told you, my Nance—" he came to her

and stood staring down at her—"I must chance it." Bringing out a worn leather purse, he pressed several coins into her hand.

"Oooh," she exclaimed, "that be more than my price."

"But no more than you deserve, my girl,'" He bent down and brushed her forehead with his lips. "I wish you might take it and go back to the country."

She looked at him wistfully. "I've often thought I might, but it wouldn't serve, goin' back."

"That is something," he said, with a hard edge to his voice and a smoldering glimmer in his dark eyes, "about which we disagree, lass."

Lady Christine Downes had enjoyed the long drive through the park which fronted De Beaufre Abbey. As usual, she found the approach to the house with its vast stretch of green lawns, bordered by trees that the late Sir Anthony de Beaufre had imported from all over the world, very impressive. However, as her post-chaise neared the intimidating stone mansion, which a seventeenth century De Beaufre had erected in place of the ancient buildings deeded to his ancestor by Henry VIII, she eyed its great oaken door and its flat roof with the battered statues apprehensively. She wished she had not consented to stay a whole week with her friend. Though she was quite fond of Bryony, she had a hankering for lively company; but Bryony, being still in mourning for Lady Honoria, would not be entertaining any other guests. Those vast gloomy halls would seem very empty. Chrissie wondered why Miss de Beaufre had chosen to incarcerate herself in this huge pile for ten mortal months. It was not the first time she had withdrawn to the country either. In the past four years she had spent considerably more time there than in her London abode, in spite of her mother's strongly expressed wishes. Yet none of Lady Honoria's many arguments had moved her daughter to compliance.

Chrissie shook her head, recalling that Bryony's preference for the Abbey had begun soon after her cousin Lucas's inexplicable disappearance. Amazingly enough, as the months had passed without any word from or about him, her friend's high spirits had completely left her, and with them had gone the young men who had so ardently pursued her; but she had not seemed to care a jot! If Chrissie had not known better, she would have suspected Bryony of pining for a lover. But since she had been the recipient of all Bryony's confidences on that score, she knew well enough that she had never considered Mr. Bardine as other than a very close and dear friend. It was her private belief that she had looked upon him as a second father. Bryony had been considerably cast down after Sir Anthony's death, and the probable demise of Lucas Bardine had recalled to mind that earlier grief, except that she had said more than once that she could not believe him dead. Yet, as Lady Honoria, Stephen and the late Sir Bertram Bardine had all insisted, how could it be otherwise, when he had been absent so long that he was quite forgotten by all except Bryony and, of course, Sir Stephen. The latter more than ever had reason to be grateful to Lucas, since upon his grandfather's death early in 1815, he had inherited the title and the extensive Bardine holdings.

Though she would never have dared to breathe such an opinion to Bryony, Chrissie was extremely glad that it was Stephen Bardine who was the new Baronet. He looked the part, being even more devastatingly handsome than he had been when she first met him—lucky Bryony to be betrothed to so charming a man! Lady Honoria had arranged that, it being her dearest and last wish, and very wise of her, too, since it was evident that Sir Stephen worshipped Bryony, even though she was no longer the same radiant girl she had been when they had first met.

Chrissie shuddered slightly. Twenty-one going on twenty-two had once seemed a great age to her but having arrived at it, she felt as young as ever and thought that she looked it, as well; but if Bryony were not Sir Stephen's intended bride, she might easily have been "on the shelf." Chrissie wished that the period of mourning were at an end and Bryony wed. Marriage must certainly restore her spirits for, as Chrissie could attest, it had benefits she had never envisioned during her innocent maidenhood. Indeed, it was most marvelously exciting! She thought of dear Alfred with a little pang—it was only because he was going off to Ireland on family business that she was spending the week with Bryony, and she would miss him sorely.

There was a tap on the carriage door. Looking down, she found to her surprise that the vehicle had come to a stop and John, her footman, was waiting to hand her down. She blushed, saying on a laugh, "Oh, dear, I must have been lost in thought."

A few moments later, her thoughts were once more proving distracting as she stood in the main hall, embracing Bryony and saying untruthfully, "My dear, how very well you are looking." Actually, she was far too thin and pale, almost the ghost of the Bryony who had been so briefly an Incomparable and the toast of London. Moving back, Chrissie was glad that she could at least be truthful when she observed, "I am glad you are in half-mourning now. I like you so much better in violet than in black."

"I expect it is more cheerful," Bryony said with the

56

indifference of one to whom clothes have ceased to matter.

"Is it a new gown?" Chrissie eyed it critically, thinking that while its muslin material looked new, its lines were old-fashioned.

"Mrs. Sims from High Town made it for me. I expect you will think it sadly dowdy, but it serves the purpose. You are looking beautiful and . . ." She paused as a tall, dark man crossed the hall bound for the library, which lay to the left of them. "Good afternoon, Mr. Bidewell," she said.

"Good afternoon, Miss de Beaufre," he responded and went on into the library, closing the door softly behind him.

"Who might that be?" Chrissie looked after him in some surprise. "He is not a servant, is he?"

"Oh, no, he is a scholar lately arrived from Oxford. He has come to catalogue the library."

"Really? He does not look particularly scholarly," Chrissie observed, her swift glance having brought her an image of bold dark eyes and a nose which, though giving evidence of having been broken, did not detract from a singularly attractive countenance.

"Oh, but he is. Indeed, it was his notion. It seems that he is traveling through the country visiting various estates and setting their libraries in order. Mr. Richard, our agent, brought him to me, and, as it happens, his arrival was most fortuitous, for Papa's books are in a turmoil and have been since his death. Poor Lucas used to beg Mama to have them put in order. He said there were undoubtedly many rare volumes among them, but she was always putting it off. Mama was never a reader. Consequently, when this man offered his services, Mr. Richard thought it an excellent idea."

"How long has he been here?" Chrissie asked curiously.

"A little over a week," Bryony replied. "He works very hard. He is in there at all hours, but he says it will take him quite a long time to achieve the order that the collection demands. Fancy, he has already discovered a first edition of Pope."

"Um." Chrissie shrugged this interesting information away. "Where does he stay? In the servants' quarters?"

"Oh, no." Bryony looked shocked. "We have given him a chamber in the east wing. Cousin Anne was afraid he might be lonely there since it is otherwise unoccupied, but he was most grateful. I expect that in common with many scholars, his pockets are quite to let."

Chrissie glanced at the library doors. "He is quite rakish-looking for a scholar." Her dark eyes now dwelt thoughtfully on Bryony's face. "I should not like to have a stranger staying in *my* house. How do you know that some morning, you may not awaken to find all the silver plate gone."

Bryony frowned. "I think Mr. Bidewell is honest and certainly he is industrious. I cannot imagine that a thief would be so obviously a gentleman, either."

"I believe that gentlemen can also be thieves." Chrissie spoke with the authority that nearly a year of wedded bliss can give one.

"I do not believe Mr. Bidewell to be a thief," Bryony returned, refusing to defer to Lady Downes's superior wisdom; though, if she had been questioned on the subject, she could have provided no cogent reason for her stand. Her encounters with the librarian had been few and, with the exception of her delighted comments on the emergence of the Pope works, largely limited to greetings; though enjoined to do so, he did not take his meals with them.

Fortunately, Chrissie did not question her further, since the subject of the scholar's honesty was not nearly so interesting as her hostess's forthcoming nuptials with Sir Stephen Bardine.

"I glimpsed the Court on my way here," she stated by way of an elliptical introduction.

"Yes, you would." Bryony nodded. "Now I have been told to give you Cousin Anne's apologies for not coming to greet you. She is lying down and will see you at supper."

"I hope she's not ill," Chrissie felt it incumbent upon her to remark, though she would much rather have redirected the conversation to Sir Stephen.

"Oh, no, she is rather frail, as you know," Bryony explained, "and feels that she must rest in the afternoons."

"Oh." Chrissie nodded. "I did think it was odd of you, my dear, to choose such a companion, when you might have taken one of your younger cousins. I am sure that Elvira or Cornelia would have welcomed the opportunity, and both are nearer your own age."

"I cannot imagine that either would have wanted to stay here, whereas Cousin Anne finds the quiet much to her liking after her brother's vicarage which, as you know, is very noisy, given his five children. Now should you want to rest, too, after your journey?"

"Rest?" Chrissie made a little face. "I am not in the mood for resting." She looked down at her exceedingly becoming striped gown, or as much of it as was to be seen under her cloak. "I expect, however, that I must look dreadfully disheveled after such a long time in the coach. I think I will change my clothes and then we must talk. I have so much to tell you!"

"And I am eager to listen," Bryony smiled. "I shall have Maggie show you your chamber, then you can join me in the music room for tea. The afternoon sun floods it, if you remember, and it is very cheerful." She put an arm around her friend's waist. "I am glad you have finally found the time to come, Chrissie. It will be so pleasant having you here for an entire week."

"For me as well," Lady Downes agreed, deciding in that moment that she had a mission, and that was to coax her friend back to London, if only for a month, so that she could buy her bride clothes as well as other *ensembles* that would make her look more like herself. Certainly Bryony owed that much to the man who would soon be her husband.

An hour later, seated in the charming music room, which, with its robin's-egg-blue walls and white ceilings etched and emblazoned with goddesses and garlands after the Adam style, was quite the prettiest chamber in the house, Chrissie regarded her friend with some relief. In these surroundings she seemed much more her old self and Chrissie concluded that it might have been the dimness of the hallway that had made her appear so faded, for the sun brought out the streaks of gold in her hair; and if her complexion was devoid of the roses which had once enhanced her cheeks, it was still a lovely color. Unfortunately, there was no doubt but that the sparkle that had once illumined her eyes was missing and with it her once-vaunted zest for life. Chrissie, delivering an enraptured account of the wonderful ball given by the Prince Regent at Carlton House the previous month, was disappointed to see that she had failed to arouse her friend's interest. Bryony seemed equally unenthusiastic about a description of the Queen's Birthday Celebration, which, for economic reasons, had been combined with a Thanksgiving for the Blessings of Peace ceremony in January. The news that Beau Brummell had fallen from grace and was sadly in debt was another *on-dit* which stirred no more concern than the latest scandal about Lord Byron, who had shocked society and his poor wife with a convulsion resulting from viewing Edmund Kean's over-realistic fit of madness in a play entitled *A New Way to Pay Old Debts*. "He is also called a secret Satanist," Chrissie confided, "and I can quite believe that, for he does have the face of a fallen angel."

"How might he be called a 'secret' Satanist if everyone knows about it?" was Bryony's slightly bored response. She added, "I have met Lord Byron and I think he is overfond of posing."

Such a response was certainly very daunting for one whose earnest desire was to entice Bryony back to wicked but exciting London; but then, she was seized with what she knew must be an ideal opening for the subject at hand. "The Princess Royal will be married next month," she stated.

"Yes." Bryony nodded. "The news has even reached Shropshire; to Prince Leopold of Coburg, I believe."

"Yes, and we will have a place in the chapel," Chrissie told her importantly. "And no doubt Alfred will be able to secure one for you, also. He is a very good friend of Prinny's. You must come. It should be a lovely wedding. Prince Leopold is quite divinely handsome and charming, too. I was presented to him at Carlton House . . . and Princess Charlotte is beautiful, not a bit like her wretched mama, for whom Alfred has not the least degree of respect or sympathy since he says she is horridly fat and ill-kempt as well as shockingly lascivious." She blushed. "Though I expect I should not be talking about such matters with an unmarried lady, and besides, it is away from the point. You will stay with us, Bryony, for I am sure you will not want to go to the trouble of opening your

London house and you will be able to buy your bridal garments and . . ."

"My bridal garments," Bryony interrupted, looking at her in almost an affrighted manner.

"You will be out of mourning by then," Chrissie said. "Is not the wedding supposed to take place at the end of June? That was my understanding. How is dearest Stephen? Will we be seeing much of him this week?"

"No." Bryony shook her head. "He is on the continent. He left a month ago. He had business in Paris, I believe."

"Oh," Chrissie said disappointedly. "I was quite looking forward to seeing him. Such a charming man. Will you ever forget how kind he was when poor Lucas vanished? Despite the fact that he had everything to lose, he insisted that your grandfather hire Bow Street Runners to trace him. Your mother told me more than once what a prop he later became to Sir Bertram."

"Yes." Bryony stared out of the window. "He was very good."

"When will he be returning?"

"In his last letter, he told me that it would be a fortnight."

"Oh." Chrissie smiled. "Then he will be here for the Princess's wedding. I knew he would not want to miss it. He is a particular friend of the Regent, you know. Oh, Bryony, my dear, I can hardly wait until you are a married lady, too. It is such utter, utter bliss."

"Chrissie," Bryony said in a low voice, "I wish you would not speak of it yet. June is nearly two months away."

Chrissie's eyes widened. "But that is a very short time, my dearest and—"

"Chrissie, please," Bryony protested, a harried expression on her countenance.

"Oh." Chrissie threw her an arch glance, "I do believe you are nervous. I myself was utterly terrified for the two months before I was wed to Alfred. There were times when I did not even like him."

Bryony regarded her with an almost painful intensity, "Were there really?" she whispered.

"Oh, bless you, yes," Chrissie giggled. "Indeed, I simply clung to Mama and Papa. I was dreadfully afraid of being married, though I cannot remember why. It is a wonder that Alfred retained his patience. But now—" her eyes glowed—"I have never regretted a second of it. Indeed, I love him more with every passing hour . . . and a married woman has so much more freedom, too. You are fond of Stephen, are you not?"

Bryony hesitated. "I expect I am," she said finally. "Only . . ." She hesitated again.

"Only what?" Chrissie prompted.

"I do not know," she said in a low voice. "Perhaps I ought not to be married."

"What can you mean?" Chrissie stared at her in astonishment.

"Some women are quite happy not being wed."

"What women? And do not tell me you are speaking about your Cousin Anne, when I know for a fact that she was betrothed to a gentleman who was killed in India."

"I was not speaking of Cousin Anne. I was thinking of the authoress Jane Austen. Cousin Anne met her in Bath and says she seemed quite content with her single state."

"An authoress!" Chrissie chortled. "But an authoress

is not a woman, at least not such an one as you or me. Oh, I know you like to scribble, Bryony—but you're not serious."

"I . . . might be," Bryony said cautiously, giving her friend a sidelong glance. "You must know that I have been doing a great deal of reading since I have been here, and shall no doubt be inspired to do much more once Mr. Bidewell has set the library to rights. Who knows, I may yet try my hand at . . . a novel."

"Oh, my dearest Bryony!" Chrissie's tone was gently condescending. "That little hand was never meant to stain itself with ink. It must be given into the keeping of Sir Stephen Bardine." Looking into her friend's unhappy face, she added a trifle apprehensively, "You cannot be meaning to cry off, my dear, not when Stephen loves you so much?"

Bryony leaped to her feet and took a turn around the room. "You know," she said finally, "that I *may* not cry off. I gave Mama a solemn promise on her deathbed that I should wed him. We joined hands. . . ."

"Yes, I do know that," Chrissie acknowledged. "And I am truly glad that your nature is such that you are constrained to abide by that promise, Bryony, because I can tell you from my own experience that you will never regret it. Believe me, my dear, your mama knew what she was about."

FOUR

On an afternoon four days after Chrissie's arrival, Bryony, coming down the stairs into the hall, sighed to herself. Her friend, informed that they were going to drive to a nearby fair, had gone to change her gown, something she did two or three times a day, whether there was a reason or not. Bryony heaved another sigh. Though she had looked forward to Chrissie's visit with considerable anticipation, it was disheartening to realize how very much she longed for it to be at an end. From that very first afternoon, the prospect of a week spent in her company had palled. Of course, she was generous enough to admit that this was due less to Chrissie than to her own state of mind. Much to her surprise, she had found herself bored by town gossip. From the distance of miles and months, tales of the people and events that had once held considerable interest for her, now seemed singularly frivolous and empty. Nor had she anything with which to entertain her friend since nothing much happened at the Abbey. One could scarcely discuss the books one had read or the horseback riding one had done or Cousin Anne's singular success in the cultivation of the Amelia and the Great Maiden's Blush roses or the attempt at a novel which had occupied and was continuing to occupy one's attention in the early morning hours and in the evenings as well, for none of these subjects held any interest for Chrissie. Consequently, she could produce no arguments to defend an existence her friend had not hesitated to condemn as "intolerably tedious and fearfully dull." Having armed herself with this conclusion, she had redoubled her efforts to wean Miss de Beaufre away from the country, elaborating upon matters already described and, in Miss de Beaufre's estimation, worn to a veritable bone.

Particularly irritating to her was Lady Downes's constant extolling of the married state as personified by Lord Alfred, whom Bryony remembered as a fairly foolish youth whose observations upon life never exceeded the commonplace. Furthermore, she could not appreciate Chrissie's constant references to Sir Stephen Bardine, whose enthusiastic advocate she had become. Until she had appeared, it had been Bryony's custom to dwell upon her pending nuptials as little as possible. The fact that Sir Stephen spent a great deal of time away from the Court had been a blessing to her; for though she was, as she had told Chrissie, fond of him and grateful for his support during her mother's final, protracted illness, the idea of being his wife weighed heavily upon her. She had no real reason for her state of mind. He was charming and obviously very much in love with her. Yet when she was with him she felt uneasy, and it was a sensation that, rather than decreasing with time, had increased. She did not understand it. She wished she might discuss it with someone—with Lucas. Lucas was very perceptive. He could have advised her.

"Oh," she whispered. "I do miss him so much, so much. What could have happened to him?"

She sighed. Though in four years that question had ceased to torment her as much as it had in the beginning, from time to time it arose to plague her; and, again, she could not discuss it with anyone. Much to her resentment, she knew her mother had been actually relieved that Lucas was no longer around to occupy her time; and, though Stephen had certainly been most sympathetic and concerned, she guessed it was difficult for him not to be pleased at a turn of events which had elevated him to a vast inheritance and a title.

As for Chrissie, she had always mocked at Lucas; and, ironically enough, since she had arrived, Bryony's longing for him had been reactivated. It would have been fun to exchange views about Chrissie's matronly self-importance! Oh, there were so many things they might have talked about. Indeed, if he had been at the Court, she might have shown him her precious manuscript. He never would have derided her "literary pretensions," he . . . Her thoughts suddenly came to an end as she heard Chrissie's light familiar step on the stairs. Even though they were due to leave soon, she did not want to see her friend at this precise moment. She darted across the hall and cravenly whisked herself into the library, closing the door behind her with a bang that was followed almost immediately by the sound of falling books.

She looked around and met the somewhat flustered gaze of Mr. Bidewell, who was stationed on top of the library stairs, which he had wheeled to the center of the vast chamber. Below him lay three volumes which, she guessed, he must have been arranging when she entered. "Oh," she said contritely, "I must have alarmed you. I am sorry." She hurried to the stairs and bent to retrieve the books as he scrambled down from his perch.

"I beg you not to trouble yourself, Miss de Beaufre," he said, kneeling quickly to gather them.

Bryony noticed for the first time that though his hands were well-shaped, they were very rough and calloused with scarred backs and two nails flattened as if from a heavy blow. She was startled. They seemed more the hands of a common laborer than those of one who had spent his days in the peaceful confines of a university library. Even as this thought crossed her mind, she met his eyes and was further startled to find them full of an odd, mocking light, as if he had guessed and was for some reason amused by the questions that the sight of them must have raised in her mind. She recalled Chrissie's suspicions as to his honesty but, she decided, almost defiantly, they were as foolish as her other opinions. Rising, she said determinedly, "I cannot tell you, Mr. Bidewell, how pleased I am that you have come to set the library in order."

Getting to his feet and setting the books on a step of the library stairs, he said, "You are most kind, Miss de Beaufre."

"I expect," she pursued, "that you must believe me sadly remiss in not attending to it before."

"I am glad you did not," he returned. "Else there would have been nothing for me to do."

"Oh!" she exclaimed. "I'd not thought of that. I am glad, too." She was suddenly and uncomfortably aware that she was blushing. "I . . . I mean that you seem uncommonly knowledgeable as to the disposition of the volumes. Perhaps another man might not have been. One has the impression that you are fond of the work."

"I do not consider it work to be once more among these volumes." For some reason, he himself reddened and said hastily, "It is a notable collection, Sir Anthony . . . de Beaufre was a well-known bibliophile."

"Oh, was he?" Her eyes lighted. "I was not aware that he enjoyed that reputation. But in those days, I mean when Papa was alive, I had not acquired such a taste for reading . . . though Lucas often told me I should take advantage of my opportunities. I expect I was rather heedless then." She gave him an embarrassed look. "I forget . . . you do not know to whom I am referring. Lucas was my second cousin. I wish you might have known him. He had a wonderful library at the Court."

"The court?" Mr. Bidewell questioned.

"His estate—it used to march with ours."

"Used to?" There was a certain sharpness to Mr. Bidewell's tone. "And now . . . no longer?"

"Oh, yes, it still does, but Lucas is not there any more. The estate has passed to his cousin, Sir Stephen Bardine, who was next in line." She sighed. "I do miss Lucas . . . he was my very good friend."

"He's dead then," Mr. Bidewell asked.

"He must be. It has been four years . . . four years this April. It was in 1812 that it happened."

"What happened?" he asked curiously.

She shook her head, and in retrospect was back in Convent Garden again, staring at that empty chair, which during the course of a long evening had remained unoccupied. "He never arrived," she murmured, half to herself. Then meeting his startled gaze, she explained hastily, "My cousin . . . disappeared. No one knows what happened to him. My fiancé, Sir Stephen, did his very best to find him, but to no avail. It was at his instigation that Sir Bertram hired the Bow Street Runners. Sir Bertram Bardine was his grandfather—Stephen's, too. He was terribly disturbed about it, but he thought the Runners would not be of much use and he was right. It . . . it was as though poor Lucas had vanished into thin air."

"It would seem to me," Mr Bidewell said matter-of-factly, "that there is a very simple explanation for that. He must have been set upon by thieves and murdered. Such occurrences are not unusual in London—I presume it happened in London?"

She nodded miserably. "Yes, and that is what Mama, Sir Bertram and the Runners all believed, but still . . ."

"You did not agree with them?" he asked curiously.

"No. He was known to have taken a hackney that afternoon. That was very odd in him. He never used such conveyances. He had his curricles and post-chaises made especially for him. He was . . . rather large, you see. Yet that day, he asked his man to order him a hackney. He must have had some sort of a special appointment. . . ." She sighed. "If only he had told someone where he was going or whom he was meeting, possibly that person might have been able to shed some light on the matter. But it does not do to dwell on it, I expect. He is gone and I must assume that he is dead."

"It would seem to be the logical assumption," Mr. Bidewell agreed gravely.

Bryony raised a woeful face to his. "Do you know, Mr. Bidewell," she said with a sudden burst of passion, "I have come to *hate* logic." She blushed. "But I—I am keeping you from your task. I must not do that. I pray you will excuse me." With a strained little smile she hurried from the room.

The man who had ironically rechristened himself

Orion Bidewell—the first name after the constellation of the Hunter, which he had often seen from the deck of the *Eagle,* the second because its implications had afforded him some wry amusement—made no attempt to resume the work Bryony had interrupted. Moving to a chair, he sat down, staring frowningly at the floor. His conversation with Miss de Beaufre had proved confusing and unsettling.

In the fortnight he had spent at the Abbey, he had almost managed to convince himself that his feelings for the girl, who, as he had prayed she might, looked upon him with no flicker of recognition in her limpid blue eyes, closely equated the hatred he entertained for Sir Stephen Bardine—Stephen, who had neatly deprived him of his estates, his title and, in a sense, Bryony. That his feelings for her had undergone a change on the day of that disappearance—which, somewhat to his surprise, still appeared to distress her—made little difference. In the years of his travail he had remembered her with affection, if not with the thwarted passion of the obese Mr. Lucas Bardine. But, to return and learn from the talkative host of the Crown and Scepter, a tavern much frequented by servants from both the Court and the Abbey, that not only had Stephen inherited, but that he was engaged to the lovely Miss Bryony de Beaufre, had shocked and enraged him. It was a damnable situation!

His lips curled as he recalled how he had meant to exact his revenge on Stephen before enlisting his grandfather's aid in reestablishing himself, but now, aside from Bryony, there was no one who could help him prove his claim. Though he had moved about in society, he had had no close friends, only acquaintances; and, faced with his radically changed appearance, not one of these could be counted on to believe his incredible story. Even if they had consented to see him, which, in itself was doubtful, given his garments—now considerably shabbier than when he had bought them, the weather encountered on the outside of a stagecoach not being conducive to preserving their initial freshness—they would merely have laughed and deemed him an impostor.

There had been Mr. James, his man of business, one who had served his grandfather, but he had died even before Sir Bertram. Everyone who might have helped him was either dead or gone from the district. Further inquiries at the tavern had brought him the information that his cook had taken a position somewhere in the North, while the rest of his former staff at the Court had been dispersed or retired for, unfortunately, his servants had always been elderly, having worked for his parents as well as himself —he never having had the heart to dismiss anyone. He ground his teeth. How easy he had made it for Stephen to assert and maintain his claim! He had no papers, nothing to establish his identity. His only hope of regaining his lost inheritance was to force Stephen to confess his guilt— and how might he do that? Under other circumstances, he would not have hesitated to approach Bryony and unleash those confidences which only they had shared.

He rose and moved back and forth across the floor, pondering their recent conversation. She had spoken of the late Lucas Bardine with an affection that called to mind that old friendship. Could he possibly explain . . . ? He shook his head, muttering, "No, do not be a fool!"

He, who had trusted the whole world once, could believe in no one—not even Bryony, least of all Bryony, who was engaged to his cousin and would, if challenged, naturally bestow her loyalty on the man she would soon wed. Yet how could he stand by and watch her become the wife of one who was little better than a murderer? He scowled. It was the first time that this particular question had crossed his mind and he did not welcome its arrival. He could not concern himself with her woes. If he were unable to intervene in that situation during the weeks before the wedding, so be it. His revenge must take precedence over all else! He absently caressed the arm where, in a fit of something perilously close to madness, he had had the V tattooed. True, he had been foxed at the time, but not that foxed! It had been a symbol of his frustration and his fury—emotions which had increased threefold! Yet—and here his scowl was replaced by a bitter smile—he had made some progress. His presence at the Abbey was due entirely to his own ingenuity and his willingness to take a risk; and certainly it had been a step in the right direction. It had given him a place to live and money to buy such necessities as he required, the while it afforded him the opportunity to further his plans. Meanwhile, he would remain unobtrusive and . . . bide well. He strode back to the library steps, but as he mounted them he heard once more the longing in her voice as she had spoken of the late Lucas Bardine.

"No matter," he whispered, "let him stay 'late.' She has chosen to love the man she calls Sir Stephen Bardine . . . and she has lost something in looks. No doubt she is pining for marriage with him . . . so let her share his fortunes or the lack of them!"

It was one of those mornings when a small breeze chivvied a covey of puffy white clouds across the sun, alternately lightening and darkening the crooked streets of Paris. A plump man in a dark suit, standing at a tall window, turned his disgruntled gaze down on those streets, muttering, "Damn ugly lot o' frogs." Turning away he fixed his eyes on the gentleman who lay in a wide tumbled bed, adding, "Though I will say that your little ladybird's a pretty bit o' muslin. Wot're you goin' to do wi' 'er once yer wed to Miss Bryony de Beaufre?" Mr. Oliver Platt bestowed a sly wink at a crumpled pillow next to that wadded under his nephew's head.

Sir Stephen Bardine raised his eyebrows, "I shall curtail my visits to Paris once we are wed. There'll be no need for them."

"Miss de Beaufre's not a patch on Yvonne when it comes to looks," his uncle remarked. "Never saw nobody go down so fast."

"No matter . . . she is a lady of high degree with an estate which will be absorbed into mine."

"And a dowry which will be absorbed by me," his uncle grinned.

"As we have long agreed. You need not continue to remind me. You'll have the best part of it once the knot is tied." Sir Stephen gave his uncle a chill glance. "And then you'll be free to go where you choose and do as you like and refrain from hanging around my neck like a damned anchor!"

"An anchor drags ye to the bottom o' the sea, nephew, an' I've lifted ye up to the topsails." Mr. Platt grinned, revealing a mouthful of yellow broken teeth.

"Very well, you have and have had my . . . deepest gratitude," Stephen growled.

"And why cannot I have more money from your estate? It is yours—why must I wait for this damned dowry?"

"And why must I continue to explain that much of that inheritance is invested in funds, and since I am using the firm that handled Sir Bertram's affairs, I should be questioned, especially if I did not invest it?"

"You might change firms."

"God in heaven, how many times must I tell you that that would only give rise to further questions? I do not want questions!"

"And I tell you that no one suspects you."

"Now. But they might, were I to make any untoward moves."

"The man is gone, forgotten, dead." Mr. Platt said.

"But he did not die aboard the *Eagle*," Sir Stephen pointed out. "You yourself told me of Briggs's communication."

"Then 'e died when it sunk . . . or 'e died in prison. We've not 'eard from 'im, 'ave we? Never fear, 'e's a corpse all right. 'E was near beaten to a pulp not long afore the boat sunk. That were enough to break 'is spirit."

"I would it had killed him," Sir Stephen muttered. "I should have seen to it in the beginning."

" 'Oo was it told you that?" Mr. Platt reminded him. "But no, you was all for rubbin' 'is nose in misery. If I'd 'ad my way, the fishes'd've made a meal o' 'im an' you could've gi' me the money right off."

"You will get it soon enough," his nephew said wearily. "I will be seeing Bryony in a week's time and we'll set the date." He smiled then, as a small, fiery-headed girl in a thin green nightdress came drifting into the room. She gave Mr. Platt an indifferent stare, then smiled beguilingly at Sir Stephen and slipped into the bed, langorously twining herself about him. He said meaningfully, "I will see you later, Uncle."

"So be it . . . an' I tell you, not a patch," Mr. Platt averred as he strolled from the room.

"What does he say?" the girl asked in French.

"He says that you are very beautiful," Stephen returned in the same language and pressed a kiss upon her parted lips, raising his head to whisper, "and I might add, my dear Yvonne, that I am in complete agreement."

The week was up and Chrissie gone. Bryony, seated at her desk, heard the clock in the hall strike hálf the hour of ten and thought she should be undressing for bed, but she was not tired. She bent over her manuscript and wrote another line. She was describing a ball to which her heroine had been invited and she was basing that description on one of Chrissie's depictions of a Carlton House entertainment; but on reading it over again she found it not to her liking. It seemed dull and lifeless. It did not have that little fillip of spice with which Chrissie was wont to imbue most of her descriptions—that insidious suggestion that more was happening than met the eye. She frowned and bit her lip, trying to forget what her friend had whispered before she left. It concerned Mr. Bidewell, for whom she had conceived an odd dislike as well as an unfounded distrust, though she was sure that Chrissie would have denied hotly that it was unfounded.

"Do you speak with that young man in there often? I should not," she had said on finding Bryony, a volume in hand, emerging from the library on an afternoon three days before her departure. . . .

"Why not?" Bryony asked in surprse.

"I find him very sinister," Chrissie whispered. Hooking her arm in Bryony's, she pulled away from the library door and into the drawing room across the hall.

"Sinister?" Bryony said as Chrissie closed the door. "I cannot think why you should come to that conclusion."

"You've not noticed his sly, sidelong glances then?"

"Sly, sidelong glances!" Bryony laughed. "Generally,

when I have seen him, his eyes have been fully fastened on one or another of the library shelves." She held up the volume. "Fancy, this is a 1660 edition of Spenser's *The Faerie Queene*. I cannot imagine how Papa came by it, and it would have been quite lost to view had not Mr. Bidewell discovered it back of some other books on one of the highest shelves. It is in excellent condition. Look at the lovely binding."

Chrissie bestowed not so much as a glance on the find. "Your Cousin Anne says she has invited him to take his meals with you, but that he has refused."

"Surely that is no reason to believe him sinister!" Bryony exclaimed.

"He seems to avoid us. Where does he go after he leaves the library?"

"That need not concern us," Bryony said, guessing that in lieu of any real scandal at the Abbey, Chrissie was trying to invent one.

A second later her friend strengthened this opinion by saying, "Have you ever noticed his hands? They seem hardly those of a gentleman."

"I expect," Bryony retorted tartly, "that he has had to work at other pursuits. He is not wealthy, else he should not need to go through the country seeking a position."

"I believe you like him," Chrissie accused. "I wonder what Stephen would think, having a man of his sort under your roof?"

"He would think that I had hired him to catalogue the library," Bryony answered coolly. "And as for liking him, I have scarcely spoken to him save when he has shown me a book he has deemed valuable."

That was the end of the discussion, but on the morning that she was due to leave, Chrissie came in to sit at the end of Bryony's bed, quite as she had been wont to do in the days before she became Lady Downes. She resembled the old Chrissie Lawton, too, with her eyes big and brimming with undisclosed confidences, which, in those faraway days, had generally concerned the gentlemen for whom she had a particular penchant.

"I have not wanted to tell you this," she began mendaciously since it was only too obvious that she was eager to unburden herself of whatever information she meant to impart.

"What have you not wished to tell me?" Bryony asked—remembering now that she had been reluctant to provide the expected response, reluctant to know what Chrissie wanted to tell.

"It concerns your . . . librarian."

Thinking about it, Bryony was aware that she had guessed that before Chrissie had spoken. "What have you not wished to tell me about Mr. Bidewell?" she asked in a chill voice.

"The other night . . . the moon was so bright and my girl had not yet drawn the curtains, and so I went to do so, and on looking into the garden I saw this figure. . . . It looked almost ghostly in the dark, but as it came closer I recognized it as that of Mr. Bidewell. He was pacing up and down as if he were deep in thought."

"Probably because he *was* deep in thought."

"Wait!" Chrissie's black eyes widened. "Let me tell you the whole of it. He went on pacing. Then suddenly, he looked up and the moonlight fell full upon a countenance that was distorted with anger. He . . . he looked, indeed, as if he were planning murder most foul!"

"Murder most foul!" Bryony repeated, laughing. "Because he was walking about at night and frowning? I think you have read too much of Mrs. Radcliffe, Chrissie!"

Chrissie's stare was affronted. "I do not read Mrs. Radcliffe, at least not since I have been married. Alfred does not think such works suitable. He says they cannot improve the mind. I am only telling you how he appeared to me—Mr. Bidewell, I mean. Yet perhaps I might not have given it another thought had I not seen him again, last night, even later, pacing up and down in the garden."

"And did he also look murderous?"

"I did not see his face—his head was down. But then . . . he raised his fists above his head and *shook* them, as if he were in a fearful rage! I do not think you should have a man of such violent tendencies employed in your household, Bryony. You and your cousin are two women alone . . ."

"With Darby, the butler, Mary and Sally, our personal maids, Mrs. Thomas, the housekeeper, not to mention the housemaids, the under housemaids, the cook, the kitchen staff, the grooms, and the stablehands."

"I do not believe Stephen would approve," Chrissie maintained.

"Stephen has not yet the ordering of my household," Bryony reminded her.

"My dear." Chrissie moved closer to her and, reaching for her hands, held them warmly. "I beg you'll not frown at me or think me interfering. I have only your best interest at heart, believe me. You are an unmarried lady and you have chosen to incarcerate yourself in the country. Though you are three months my senior, you are yet very innocent and cannot know what dread things can happen to unprotected females. There is something about that man I *cannot* like. I have the feeling he is not what

79

he seems. And, if I were you, I should stay away from the library if you feel you must continue to retain his services—which, I shall not hesitate to say, is *most* unwise."

As she had listened, Bryony had been conscious of a growing anger. It had been difficult to maintain her self-control and to laugh lightly, shrugging away Chrissie's advice, when she had longed to tell her friend that marriage did not necessarily give her the right to pontificate about matters that did not concern her. Thinking about it now, she was still angry—angry at Chrissie and at herself, because the moon was shining through her window, and she was tempted to go into the chamber that had been alotted to Chrissie because of its pretty garden view, and see if he were once more pacing up and down in the darkness. It would be an action most unworthy of her—since certainly he had a right to pace up and down in the garden if he chose—and to be angry if he chose. She was sorry that Chrissie had noticed his rough hands. She wished that she had not shared her friend's suspicions, if only for a moment, for she liked him. Though, as she had told Chrissie, she had had very little to say to him, save for that one conversation earlier in the week. She felt comfortable with him, more comfortable than any man except Lucas, but that was ridiculous! She had known Lucas all her life and Mr. Bidewell only a fortnight, and she could not really say that she knew him, since they had had very little to say to each other. Her frown deepened. She was dwelling far too much on a person who must soon leave —for certainly, his work in the library could not last beyond a month, at the most, six weeks.

Resolutely, she turned her attention back to her manuscript, staring at her half-written page. She picked up her pen and was about to dip it into the inkwell—then she threw it down and slipped out of the room. She went to the chamber Chrissie had occupied, lingering on the threshold and eyeing the windows through which moonlight threw leafy shadows on the carpet.

It was, she knew, utterly ridiculous for her to have come, for surely he would not spend every night pacing up and down in the garden. It was amazing that Chrissie had caught him at it twice. Thinking about that, Bryony was uncomfortably positive that her friend's second viewing had come about through a protracted vigil at that window in the hopes of seeing him again and possibly fomenting trouble. Knowing Chrissie, Bryony could guess the reasons for this scrutiny. Mr. Bidewell's solitary habits must have annoyed her. Her reference to his refusal to sup with them might have been construed as a personal insult, for Chrissie was a born flirt; and Mr. Bidewell, Bryony realized with a slight shock, was extremely handsome. With all this in mind, she was tempted to return to her own chamber immediately. She took a step, but somehow it was toward, rather than away from, the window; and in a regrettably short time she was standing at it, staring at paths bordered by Cousin Anne's prized beds of Amelia roses. The light from a half-moon silvered them, but there was no tall shape to disturb the serenity of the scene. She had not expected that there would be. She was about to turn back—but then she heard a sound. Looking to the left she saw a figure kneeling by a tree, almost, she thought, as if he were searching for something or—it seemed as if Chrissie had suddenly stolen to her side and was pouring insidious hints into her unwilling ear —as if he were *burying* something . . . silver plate? She marked the tree. It was the middle one in a grouping of three. Then he arose and moved—could she describe it

81

as stealthily?—into the shadows. She waited to see if he would come again, but he did not. She lingered for a few more moments and then knew she could not rest until she had discovered what he might have buried at that tree. She found, too, that there was a throbbing in her throat and the hint of tears behind her eyes—even though, as she was quick to remind herself, there was no real evidence of his perfidy and his reasons for kneeling beside the tree might well be perfectly innocent. Still it *was* strange that he should be wandering once more through that darkened garden . . . but would it have seemed strange to her if Chrissie had not mentioned it? She shook her head. Her thoughts were becoming muddled. Moving back into her chamber, she found her cloak and dragged it about her. She took one of the candles from her desk and went softly down the stairs, opened the front door, and emerged onto the path that led to the circular driveway.

She was about to make her way to the gardens when she heard a step upon that graveled expanse and with a little frightened gasp, whirled to find Mr. Bidewell coming into view.

"Miss de Beaufre!" he exclaimed in a surprised whisper, "and with a candle! Excellent! We are well met."

"What might you be doing here?" she asked calmly, finding that for some reason her incipient fear had vanished.

"I have been walking. It is my habit on nights when sleep eludes me. And I have found a creature which needs help. I am of the opinion that it is a baby owl, but your light must settle the question." He held out his cupped hands. "Might you bring the candle closer, please?"

She hastened to obey, holding the candle over what appeared to be a mass of grey down. Then the flame was reflected in two large round dewy eyes, which blinked defensively. "Ooooh," she crooned, "it *is* an owl . . . a baby. Wherever did you find it?"

"By a tree in the garden. It must have fallen from its nest. It needs sustenance—a bit of beef scraping, perhaps."

"And a box with down or cotton wool to line it," she said. "I have cared for birds before. When I was little my Cousin Lucas and I had a sort of hostel for hurt animals, at least he did. I only helped. Come, we will go to the kitchens . . . we should find part of a prime rib in the butler's pantry."

"Very well. I must say that your arrival was most fortuitous, Miss de Beaufre."

She was glad that the quality of the light was such that he could not see the flush that warmed her cheeks. She felt it incumbent upon her to explain: "I was restless and in no mood to retire. I thought I might sit by the pool in the garden. It is very peaceful there."

"Yes, it is a pretty place," he agreed, as he followed her inside.

The kitchens seemed dark and cavernous as they entered them. The tiny flame of her candle seemed only to render them more shadowy; and she became aware that there was a certain lack of propriety in this invasion. "I . . . think we must find more candles," she said nervously.

"There are some on the table. I know for I have taken some of my meals down here," he told her. "I will bring you one and light it from yours." He moved unerringly in the direction of the table, and, after gently depositing the bird upon it, brought her a candle in a brass holder. This he ignited and set back on the table. Retrieving the owl he cradled it gently in his hands again.

Looking at it, Bryony shook her head. "Poor little creature," she murmured. "I wish we might find a way to return it to its nest.

"Yes, I wish we might. It is not pleasant to be so summarily thrust from your home."

It seemed to her that there had been an odd bitterness in his voice as he made this observation; but, on glancing at him, she read nothing in his expression save a concern for the owl.

"We must feed it." She led the way to the butler's pantry. As she had anticipated, there was a large prime rib reposing on a platter. Opening a drawer, she took out a knife and handed it to him. "Do you scrape off the beef, and I shall go upstairs and fetch a box. I have the very thing among my jewels. Should I line it with down or cotton wool?"

"Cotton wool will suffice."

"But where will we keep it? Mary, who maids me, has a horror of any kind of bird!"

"No matter," he assured her. "I shall tend it."

"You are very kind."

"I must say the same of you, Miss de Beaufre," he answered politely.

For some reason she found something almost hurtful in his response, and as she went to fetch the box she puzzled over it, and decided it was the impersonal way in which his response had been couched. Until that moment, there had been a *camaraderie* between them of which she had not actually been aware until it had been dispersed by his punctilious reply. She emitted a short, annoyed sigh. Again, she was expending far too much thought upon the man. Yet they did have something in common—a mutual love for books and a concern for the plight of small, wounded creatures. In a sense, the latter trait had surprised

84

her, for Mr. Bidewell had a hardness about him that would seem to have precluded the gentleness he had exhibited when touching the owl. In that again, she had been reminded of Lucas, who would have been equally gentle. It was odd how very much she was thinking about Lucas lately. In the past year there had been times when she had not really dwelt upon him at all; but now his image seemed larger than ever in her mind. It was almost as if, she thought with a little shiver, his ghost had returned to haunt the Abbey. . . .

Mr. Bidewell, engaged in rearranging an ancient set of Shakespeare according to date rather than category, was thinking less of the position of *Coriolanus* than he was of the owl, whose presence in his room he was beginning to regret—or, rather, *had* regretted for the past week. The bird was thriving and it had grown larger. He could envision a time when, instead of satisfying it with beef scrapings, he might need to go mouse hunting—though, by then, no doubt, it would be able to do its own foraging. It was not its dietary difficulties which concerned him the most, but the interest both Bryony and her cousin Anne had taken in the foundling. Both ladies had developed the habit of coming into the library at least once a day; and thus that which he had hoped to avoid was coming to pass. He was being drawn more into the life of the household than was safe. He was there for a purpose, which was to observe, and to plan. That his observations had come to naught was, of course, not the fault of Miss de Beaufre or her cousin. Sir Stephen Bardine was not at the Court, but still in France.

Mr. Bidewell had his suspicions about the business that occupied Sir Stephen in that country. His brief acquaintance with the present Baronet had led him to believe that reading poetry to elderly ladies and waltzing with their daughters was not the limit of his activities in the petticoat line. Certainly Paris would offer him both variety and secrecy. He grimaced. That such a man would soon wed Miss de Beaufre was proving more galling than he had anticipated. Inadvertently, he glanced at the door, then glared at *Coriolanus* and slammed it into place.

He had no business hoping that the door might open and that she would come to inquire after the health of the bird she had christened Minerva and he Jupiter, since neither had any notion of the owl's gender. It was extremely dangerous for him to cultivate Miss de Beaufre—if she should guess his identity, she might alert her lover— or would she? He was no longer sure of that. He had a feeling he could trust her. Yet . . . he had trusted Stephen Bardine. He shook his head. There had been a man aboard the *Eagle,* one Elias Briggs, whom he had also trusted— to get a letter to his grandfather. It had gone no further than the first mate, who, taking exception to his description of life aboard the ship, had ordered the flogging which had not ceased even after he had fallen unconscious in his bonds. That was the last time he had believed in anyone. And if she were to guess . . .

If he were wise, he would leave. Indeed, each day for the past week he had contemplated that move. That he had gone no further than thinking about it was a weakness in himself that he could not approve. There were, of course, valid reasons for his hesitation. He hated the idea of leaving his work unfinished. There was also the matter of where he might stay. His chamber was considerably more comfortable than anything he could afford. Yet if he were to be honest, that was not an excuse either. There had been times when he had slept in verminous dungeons, in haylofts, on the floors of abandoned huts, and even in the open fields. He . . . He tensed: the handle of the door was turning—which one of the ladies would it be? It was late for Cousin Anne; she usually rested after her noonday meal. He felt the corners of his mouth twitching into a welcoming smile, and, rather than being discovered with an expectant, even an eager look in his eyes, he hastily fixed his attention on the Shakespeare. Then his jaws tightened as a voice he had not heard in four years said with a touch of hauteur:

"You would be Mr. Bidewell?"

He had the sensation that every vein in his body had suddenly become boiling hot. Fortunately this response lasted only an instant; and, through the exercise of his admirable self-control, he was able to turn and smile the way any man in his position might smile when accosted by a stranger who was a guest in the house.

"Yes, sir, I am Mr. Bidewell," he acknowledged without a tremor to the man who stood on the threshold—the man whose handsome features, grown heavier and coarser, had haunted his dreams, and whose name had been a part of the litany of hate with which he had sent himself to sleep during those brief and terrible nights after he had awakened into agony and anonymity as one of a wretched handful of press ganged recruits in the heaving hold of *H.M.S. Eagle*. It had been a nightmare long in abating. It had been filled with a retching sickness. It had been augmented by his terror of the sea, by the itching, throbbing pain of his assaulted flesh, and by the gut-horror with which he had first viewed those lurid pictures, indelibly imprinted on chest and arm. There had been the indifferent brutality of the crew and the calculated cruelty of the officers, all of whom had jeered at his mammoth size and greeted his agonized protests and pleas to be set ashore with lip-splitting, nose-breaking, eye-blackening blows. It had been an inferno, and, plunged into its core, he had seen others, similarly captured by those marauding press gangs, die in their sickness, of harsh treatment, of fear, of maggoty rations, of fevers, and of wounds sustained in the heat of battle and negligently attended. There had been times when he had thought he, too, must die, times when he might even have welcomed death—but for the man who stood in that doorway. It had been the memory of this man's duplicity, his ingratitude, his villainy that had given him the will to survive and as his body had decreased in bulk, had strengthened and hardened, his brain had kept pace with it. He, who had been easygoing and gentle, who had found anger too much of an exertion, had entertained himself with visions of what he might do were he ever to come face to face with his cousin again. Now, staring at him from the top of the library steps, he could only smile, the while his mistrustful mind endeavored to provide reasons for Sir Stephen's presence in the library. Had it been at the behest of Bryony? Had she suspected and sent him hither to corroborate those suspicions? He said mildly, "Might I be of assistance, sir?"

Sir Stephen's stare was suspiciously penetrating. "I am Stephen Bardine and I have the honor to be engaged to Miss de Beaufre. I am recently returned from London, where I had occasion to meet with Lady Downes. She gave me to understand that my fiancée had engaged a . . . traveling librarian. I must admit that I was surprised, since I was not aware that such an occupation existed."

"Indeed, sir?" Mr. Bidewell's eyes reflected only surprise, while his mind obliged with images of Chrissie Lawton, whom he never could abide, coming into the library to stand looking provocatively up at him.

"Might you recommend me some reading matter, Mr. Bidewell?" she had said, making play with her long lashes. "I do find the evenings a bit tedious and . . . monstrous quiet, too. I should like to have some manner of literature to beguile the passing hours . . . ere I can sleep." Her eyes had been full of invitations, which he had affected not to comprehend. Now, and not for the first time, he regretted that impish impulse which had moved him to give her two volumes of the Reverend Jeremy Taylor's sermons—collectively entitled *Holy Living* and *Holy Dying*. There had been no misconstruing the enmity that had glittered in her eyes as she pettishly rejected them. It had not abated during the rest of her stay. He wondered what she might have said to Sir Stephen in London. Had she guessed his true identity? No, he was sure she had not. Though Chrissie Lawton had been Bryony's bosom friend, and often a guest at the Abbey when he had been in residence at the Court, he had always avoided her. In their happily brief encounters, the glances she had thrown at the huge Mr. Lucas Bardine had been derisive and mainly centered on his monstrous belly.

Sir Stephen said, "Have you acted in this . . . er . . . capacity in the libraries of other estates?"

"Oh, yes, sir," Mr. Bidewell assured him. "I had the honor of cataloguing the library of the Duke of Norfolk."

"The Duke of Norfolk died in November last," Sir Stephen said.

"Yes, sir," Mr. Bidewell confirmed. "A great loss, sir."

"Um . . ." Sir Stephen grunted. "It is difficult for me to understand why Miss de Beaufre should have elected to have her library set in order at this particular time. In fact, I cannot think but that your work has been for naught."

"For naught, sir?" Mr. Bidewell raised inquiring eyebrows.

"In another month—"

"Stephen!" Bryony appeared behind him. "I expected to find you awaiting me in the music room," she observed in accents which were not altogether welcoming.

"Bryony, my dear." Sir Stephen turned quickly and bowed over her hand. "How very charming you are looking, such a pleasure to see you in white instead of black. It makes me anticipate all the more the moment when . . . But as to my presence here, I pray you'll not think me officious, but on meeting dear Lady Downes in London, I was informed that you had added to your staff, and at a time when the Abbey must soon be closed."

From his perch Mr. Bidewell could see that Miss de Beaufre's slender figure had tensed. "I beg you will come with me to the music room," she said insistently. "We must not interrupt Mr. Bidewell's work."

It seemed as though Sir Stephen would protest; but then, shrugging, he bowed a second time. "As you choose, my dear." Without a glance at the librarian he disappeared from the doorway. Bryony lingered a second longer. "I do hope you have not been unduly disturbed, Mr. Bidewell," she said, with a hard edge to her voice.

He shook his head. "Not in the least, Miss de Beaufre. I was merely putting this set of Shakespeare in the proper order."

"I am glad of that," she smiled. She seemed on the point of saying something else but, evidently thinking better of it, she gave him a little nod and slipped out, closing the door gently behind her.

He was glad that she had gone. He could not have trusted himself to maintain his calm much longer in the face of his mounting anger. The sight of Sir Stephen had been enough to heat it—but it had doubled at his words and trebled as he had kissed Miss de Beaufre's hand and quadrupled at the reference to "another month," which he had had no difficulty in interpreting. In another month Sir Stephen Bardine would have wed Miss de Beaufre and, as her husband, he would have the choosing of the staff.

Mr. Bidewell's eyes grew intent. Bryony's greeting of Sir Stephen had been far from ecstatic, and it might very well be that she had resented his blatant assumption of ownership. However, she herself had given him that privilege. Once they were wed, the Hall and the Abbey would also be wedded to each other and Sir Stephen would become the ruler of an even greater domain. Yet, he could not think of that now. Sir Stephen was in residence at the Court and it was time to act . . . but how? He had yet to evolve a plan.

When he had returned from America it had seemed very simple—he would call Stephen out, give him his choice of weapons and slay him, his prowess with sword and pistol having increased to the point where he was a master of both. It was no longer so simple. Sir Stephen had money, power and prestige on his side and, as Mr. Bidewell had reluctantly decided, he dared not reveal himself. Just as officers on vessels could be bribed so could judges, and transportation to New South Wales, or even hanging could easily be his fate. There was no doubt in his mind that he must retain the identity of Orion Bidewell—but how might that impecunious scholar find the excuse to challenge the master of Bardine Court?

There was, of course, another alternative. Stephen, in his place, he was sure would not have hesitated to employ it. However, he would not contemplate the idea of out-and-out murder. What could he do? The ingenuity with which he had inserted himself into the De Beaufre establishment no longer seemed worthy of self-congratulation. Indeed, it might have been better had he remained in hiding. Yet, if becoming Mr. Bidewell had proved a complication rather than a solution, he remained determined. He was sure that, even if the means were as yet unavailable, a way would be shown him. The end for which he had doggedly survived the unrelenting hardships of the past four years was at last in sight.

FIVE

It was a yellow-grey day with a hint of rain in the air, and the pale glow invading the music room made its blue walls look dingy and its sculptured ceilings appear etched in shadow. The white gown, another effort of the village dressmaker, had hardly merited Sir Stephen's praise, for it was ill-fitting and in that light seemed dim, while its wearer's skin and hair were correspondingly dull. The quality of light was no more flattering to Sir Stephen. Scanning his face Bryony came to much the same conclusions as had Mr. Bidewell. His gain in weight was not enough to thicken his waistline, but in some odd way it had robbed his features of their refinement and caused him to look older than his years, especially now when they were marred by his heavy frown. This expression had been occasioned by Miss de Beaufre's gentle but firm reminder that she was yet the head of her household and, as such, privileged to hire whom she chose. She ended this discourse by stating with some hauteur, "You are not required to inspect my staff, Stephen."

He was silent a moment as if weighing his words. Now, replacing his frown with a conciliating smile, he said, "I am truly sorry, my dear. I am aware that I did take too much upon myself by going into the library without your permission. However, if I erred, it was only out of my concern for you. You see, I did not receive a favorable report on Mr. Bidewell from Lady Downes. She seemed to consider him an unlikely choice for your librarian."

"Since Chrissie is neither a scholar nor even much of a reader, she is hardly in the position to judge Mr. Bidewell's merits or the lack of them," Miss de Beaufre retorted.

"I had the impression that she was basing her observations on his general deportment."

"Mr. Bidewell is the most unobtrusive of men, and since Chrissie had not, to my knowledge, spent any time at all in the library, I cannot understand why she has chosen to hold him in aversion nor do I care. He has been most diligent in the task he was hired to perform and that, I believe, is what matters."

He regarded her gravely. "You are quite right, my dear, but since we are to be wed in only four weeks' time and the library transferred to the Court, it would seem to me—"

"Papa's library transferred to the Court!" she exclaimed. "Why should that happen?"

"My dear." Sir Stephen gave her a cajoling smile. "You cannot expect to dwell in two establishments at once! Naturally, I assumed that when we were wed, the

Abbey would be, of necessity, vacated and either razed or sold."

"No," she protested, "it is my home."

"But my dearest love," he said reasonably, "you will live with me at the Court."

"No," she repeated, adding in a strangled whisper, "I know we've not spoken about it, but I . . . I must tell you I cannot live at the Court."

"Cannot?" He raised his eyebrows. "Why not?"

"Because I . . . prefer it here. There's no entail any more. It ended with Papa. . . ." She clasped her hands tightly together. "I should not feel comfortable at the Court."

His gaze fastened on her clenched fingers. Moving to her, he covered them with his own hand. "Very well, my dearest love, since I live only to please you, I shall bow to your wishes." He smiled at her. "Now that we are in accord, my love, should we not discuss our approaching nuptials?" Before she could respond, he continued, "If you but knew how very happy I was to see you in your white gown, which, in my own fancy, I adorned with lace and, letting my imagination range even further afield, dropped a bridal veil upon your lovely head! Oh, Bryony, I have waited so long, far too long to possess you." He had not yet relinquished her hands and now he lifted both palms to his lips, covering them with kisses.

"Stephen . . ." She tried to pull away. "Please, it is not right. My cousin . . ."

"Damn your cousin!" he exclaimed. "Are we not plighted? Are we not nearly one?" He stared into her agitated countenance, then pulled back, saying shakily, "You must forgive me, Bryony. I am never enough in command of myself when I am with you. This year of mourning has been one of a double grief to me, a double loss. Your poor mother, whom you knew I honored and respected, and yourself, but thank God, the time of waiting is nearly at an end—such a weary round of long, long days and endless nights!" He gave her a penetrating look. "You seem disturbed, my dear. Am I frightening you? Or can it be that I have suffered alone?"

She swallowed, wishing devoutly that she might tell him that he had, but she did not want to wound him. She said in a small, unhappy voice, "It . . . has been difficult."

"Oh, my dearest, you have so relieved my mind!" he cried. "There have been terrible moments when I have feared you did not love me as much as I love you, feared that you might even wish to be released from that promise you made that night, when we joined hands in your mother's chamber." His eyes bored into hers. "You have not forgotten . . . you will abide by it, as you swore you would?"

"If . . . you still want me . . ." she murmured.

"*If!* Have you not been listening to me?" He dropped to his knees. "Bryony, Bryony, Bryony, can you know to whom I address my prayers at night?"

"Oh, please," she protested, "you must not kneel!"

"I am kneeling to my Divinity!" he said passionately.

Miss de Beaufre found her trepidation changing to annoyance. She recalled that in the days before he had been restored to his grandfather's good graces he had been an actor, and it seemed to her that there was something particularly theatrical in his present pose. Impatiently she said, "I wish you'd not be excessive, Stephen."

He arose immediately. "Can you think that I do not mean every word that I say?" he demanded reproachfully. "You are my Divinity. When we are apart, that is how I think of you. Oh, I have hated these separations

—I have been so damnably lonely. Paris is a beautiful city or, at least, so I am told, but it had no beauty for me . . . because you were not with me. To wander its streets alone—it is a cruel punishment!"

Gazing into his ardent eyes, Bryony was more than ever reminded of his background. She could almost imagine that there were footlights burning at his feet. She also wished that she was not the sole member of his audience, and was annoyed that Cousin Anne was sleeping in her chamber. A chaperone should be on hand to chaperone!

"Oh," he was continuing huskily, "you are so beautiful, Bryony. It is difficult to remain in your presence without wishing . . . but I dare not voice it."

He was exaggerating, she thought angrily, remembering her distress at the image that had stared back at her from her looking glass that very morning. She had looked too pale and she had felt amazingly old—which, of course, was not surprising, considering that her twenty-second birthday would take place at the end of June.

"You are very silent," he accused. "Oh, I should love to know what you are thinking, most exquisite of Sphinxes!"

"Sphinxes!" she repeated and was immediately visited by the inspiration she needed to divert Sir Stephen from his determined and, to her mind, increasingly tedious protestations of love. "Fancy, Stephen, the day before yesterday, Mr. Bidewell made a most felicitous discovery—a volume entitled *Pyramidographia,* which was published in the middle of the seventeenth century. It was written by John Greaves, a Professor from Oxford, who visited many of the pyramids in Egypt. Mr. Bidewell told me that he read a marvelously detailed description of the Great Pyramid at Giza in it. Mr. Greaves said it was full of bats. They were all around him when he went through it and he had only thin tapers to light his way. I cannot think of anything more horrid than to be in close quarters with bats, can you?"

"Bryony," Sir Stephen said in a muffled voice, "why are you being so cruel to me?"

"Cruel?" she repeated. "I thought you must be interested in Mr. Greaves's findings."

"I am interested only in you. Can you not see that I am suffering?" He grasped her hands again, holding them tightly. "Sometimes I think that you have no regard for me at all!"

She tensed. The diversion had not only been unsuccessful, it had made matters worse, for Stephen's grasp was heavy and hurtful. He was too close to her and he was breathing hard, as if he had just finished running a long race. There was a look in his eyes which seemed almost hungry. She had a sensation of being devoured, engulfed, absorbed into him and knew, in the back of her mind, that it was not the first time she had experienced these feelings. Yet, never before had they been so definable or his proximity so repugnant to her.

If only she had not clung so closely to him in the days after Lucas's disappearance, trying vainly to find in this other cousin traces of the comrade she had lost. In the process she had given him far too much encouragement and not, unnaturally, he had reacted with an offer. She had refused, disappointing him, but disappointing her mother even more.

"You have dismissed all your other suitors," she had croaked. "You'll end up an old maid. Furthermore, you have led Stephen to believe that you care for him. That was cruel in you, Bryony—the poor lad is much cast down." There had been a great deal more that Lady Honoria had had to say on that subject, inspired, no doubt, by just such melodramatics as Sir Stephen had just voiced to her. Her mother had always had a soft spot for him —and it had become greatly enlarged as she had neared her final illness, culminating in that moment when she had exacted that fatal promise. It had been cruel for her to use such persuasions to bend her daughter to her will, Bryony had thought at the time, but given the circumstances, given her mother's pallid face and great burning eyes, there had been no refusing her; and for the last year, Bryony had been endeavoring to accustom herself to the thought of being his bride. The fact that Stephen was so often absent had made it easier for her—but now that he was close to her again, she felt helpless and trapped. Lucas, she thought despairingly, had always freed trapped creatures and if he had been there . . . But if he had been there, she never would have been placed in this untenable position! The pressure on her hands was increasing—the trap was closing and she was at Stephen's mercy! Yet she could not let him know her fright; it would only make matters worse. Oh, that horrid promise! If there were only some honorable way that she might be released from it! She looked at him despairingly. "Please . . . let me go," she begged.

He did not heed her. Catching her in his arms, he kissed her hard on the lips. She tried to twist away but to no avail. The trap held her fast and her mouth was forcibly close against his.

"Oh, dear, dear, dear, this will not do!" said a voice from the doorway. "Stephen, no! Please, you are betrothed, I know, but such breach of conduct cannot be countenanced. It really cannot. You must release Bryony at once!"

Flushing, Sir Stephen dropped his arms and backed

away, hastily turning toward Miss Anne Seton, who looked, thought her grateful relative, not unlike an avenging angel, being tall, thin, and possessed of a nimbus-like arrangement of curly grey hair worn back from a face, which though aged, retained the remnants of that sexless beauty with which artists are wont to imbue members of the heavenly host. The resemblance was further heightened by her habit of wearing a white wool shawl back to front, its two ends trailing behind her like a pair of wings. Meeting her stern blue gaze he stuttered, "I . . . I beg your pardon, but I was carried away. Your pardon, Bryony. I pray you will give it."

She was torn by anger at him and relief at her cousin's timely intervention. It was on the tip of her tongue to avow that she would see him no more but the memory of that promise came back to stifle the words in her throat. "You have it, Stephen," she said tightly. "But I pray that you will leave me now."

"Bryony," he returned in stricken tones, "you are dismissing me?"

She shook her head, "You know I cannot do that, but please . . . will you go?"

"How may I make amends?"

"Stephen, dear boy." Miss Seton make a vague gesture with her long thin hands. "I do think you'd best leave and, uh . . . a cooling draught might be in order. I have always thought that a syllabub is most effective when the blood is . . . er . . . heated."

He shot her an annoyed glance, but said politely, "I will keep your advice in mind, Miss Seton." Turning back to Bryony, he continued, "I will go, my dearest, and again I pray that you will forgive me." Bending over her hand, he brushed it with his lips, saying throatily, "I shall bid you farewell and I promise you on my honor that I shall not act in so importunate a manner again." Without waiting for her response, he strode from the room.

"Oh, oh, dear!" Bryony sank down on an adjacent settee.

"Child . . ." Miss Seton hovered over her anxiously. "Such a lack of propriety. I do not know what to make of it! In my day a young man would have been ostracized for conducting himself so boldly. Of course, you are plighted, but moderation should be of paramount . . ." She stopped, startled, as Bryony abruptly rose to her feet.

"Excuse me, dearest Anne, but I think I must exercise Albion."

"Ah," Miss Seton nodded, "perhaps that would be wise. I have learned from my own experiences that riding can be very soothing when the mind is disquieted. But I must adjure you not to remain away too long. My arm is aching, the one I broke in the fall down the stairs twenty winters ago. Can you imagine that it was such a long time ago? It healed very nicely. We had an excellent doctor . . . but still when it is due to rain, there is an ache in it . . . so I should keep that in mind."

Bryony, who was used to Miss Seton's lengthy discourses on matters of very little moment, gave her a hug. "I shall be back in good time, I assure you. And let me add that I am very grateful that you arrived when you did."

"Are you, my love?" Miss Seton inquired a trifle anxiously. "Though he did show a deplorable lack of manners, I have often thought that young people are not always obliged by such interruptions, though of course they ought to be. . . ."

Bryony, anticipating another discourse, brought it to an abrupt end by saying as she made a strategic exit, "Dearest Cousin Anne, rest assured that I meant what I told you, every word!"

Stephen, striding into the main hall of the Court, was not pleased to hear from Burton, his butler, that his groom, who had been granted leave to remain in London, ostensibly to buy some horses at Tattersall's, had unaccountably returned and begged that his employer see him immediately on his return.

"Very well," Stephen snapped. "Let him come to the library."

"I believe, sir, that Mr. Platt is already in the library," the butler said impassively, but with a certain haughty disdain in his eyes.

Sir Stephen's displeasure was heightened when, on coming into the room in question, he found Mr. Platt seated at the wide desk which the late Lucas Bardine had had made to his order, and a goblet filled with gin near him. "Damn you," he frowned, "we had agreed that you would act according to your station. And look what you've done!" Lifting the glass, he exposed a wet, discolored ring marring the desk's polished surface.

Retrieving the glass, his uncle glared up at him. "It don't please me to be summoned by yon 'igh-an-mightiness. And there may be no need for you to be so particular about your possessions." He glanced about the large, airy room with its beautiful paneling and its high shelves of books in their shining leather bindings. "Might not be yours much longer, Nephew."

Stephen's eyes narrowed. "What are you hinting at, you old vulture? Is it money you're wanting? I am not yet reduced to selling my furniture."

"Like I was sayin', might not be *your* furniture, Stephen, lad. 'Eard somethin' very interestin' when I was in London, it's wot brought me back 'ere 'ell for leather. Damned rough ride, it were, too, like to shake me teeth from me jaws."

"Something interesting? What have you heard?" Stephen paled. "You haven't had word of Lucas?"

"Maybe so, maybe not. 'Eard as 'ow you was visitin' up at the Abbey . . . seein' Miss Bryony, eh? I 'ope all is goin' well in that direction." He cast a knowing glance at his nephew's face. "Though from the looks of ye, I'd say as 'ow there might be white water in the stream o' love. 'Ow do you like that for poetry, me boy?"

Stephen said sharply, "Will you explain what you mean?"

"I 'appened to 've dropped by me old lodgin's— sometime there's a letter for me—an' then I stopped by Mabe's gin shop an' 'ad a chat wi' im."

"And then?" Sir Stephen prompted.

"Well, Mabe told me as 'ow there were a cove a-lookin' for me. Seafarin' man 'oo were askin' for an Oliver 'oo's other name 'e thought was Platt. Thin, dark fellow 'e were, wi' a strange way of talkin'—that's wot struck Mabe, the way 'e spoke." He paused, frowning at Sir Stephen.

"How did he speak?"

"Like one o' *them,* Mabe said . . . a swell, which surprised 'im, for 'e weren't dressed like no swell an' it looked like 'e'd done 'is share o' 'ard work in 'is time. It was only 'is palaver. It came to me that maybe yer cousin Lucas ain't as dead as we'd like 'im to be."

Stephen shook his head. "It's not possible," he muttered. "A seafaring man . . . that could not be Lucas. It might have been one of your old clients."

"I don't recollect that any o' them talk like a swell," Mr. Platt said. "An' ye forget it's four years since we set 'im afloat. 'E's ad some trainin' in the fine art o' sailin' since then. I wish I'd been able to find the doxy wot walked out wi' im that night."

103

"Doxy?"

" 'E went off wi' one of them as 'angs around the shop. Nance, 'er name was, but when I went lookin' for 'er, she must've been occupied." Mr. Platt gave him a knowing grin.

"Damn, why didn't you wait and see her?" Sir Stephen exclaimed.

"Thought I'd best get back to you wi' my tale. Wasn't sure as if it amounted to anythin' an' wasn't sure if it didn't . . . which is why I tell ye, ye'd better tie the knot wi' the little heiress as soon as ever ye can, because it might be 'is nibs'll be comin' back to claim wot's rightly 'is."

"If he comes back, which I very much doubt, he will be able to claim nothing," Stephen said coldly. "I have inherited the title and the estates. I doubt very much if he would be able to pay the fees which would enable him to employ an advocate—and if he does show himself in this part of the world—I think we can arrange a more permanent method of despatching him. Was there anyone else to whom you spoke concerning this man?"

"Couldn't find nobody. Only the whore'd know, she's the last wot seen 'im."

"And how long ago was that?" Stephen asked.

Mr. Platt shrugged. "Mabe weren't sure, 'e thought a week or more."

Stephen glared at him. "You should have waited to see that girl."

"Whyn't you see 'er yerself, "Mr. Platt suggested, "if you're so interested?"

Sir Stephen gazed at him thoughtfully. "It's what I will do—what we will do," he amended. "Yet I cannot imagine my fastidious and virginal Cousin Lucas with a whore."

"Like I said, it's been four years an' 'e's been sailin' in some rough seas . . . though it don't 'ave to've been 'im."

"No, and probably it was not, but I am taking no chances . . . and this girl would know."

" 'E might not 'ave given 'er 'is callin' card," his uncle said.

"Damn, where's your brain, man!" Sir Stephen exploded. "What about the tattoos?"

"By all that's 'oly, fancy me forgettin' them," Mr. Platt muttered. "You got a good 'ead on your shoulders, Stevie. Always said so. When do we leave?"

"Immediately!" Sir Stephen rasped.

By four in the afternoon the promised rain had materialized and over the trees broad pillows of mist rolled, losing their moisture in small, penetrating drops which seemed much wetter than their larger equivalents. Mr. Bidewell, watching countless rivulets form and roll down the library windows, stared at them moodily, shaking his head. He had felt the need to walk off his interior angers. In his tortured days at sea he had found some solace in the strenuous tasks that had been his lot. Even in the beginning, when his unused muscles had been throbbing knots of agony and his soft flesh bruised and bleeding, the exertion had helped take his mind from his hapless situation. To have dwelt upon it too long would have left him in a despair so profound as to have rendered him inactive. He had seen two other victims of the press gang, landsmen like himself, so overcome by misery that even the harsh treatment they had received from their superiors had failed to rouse them. One had gone mad and the other had drowned himself. Lucas Bardine had, however, been able to fix his attention on the swabbing of the deck, on the mending of sails, and on the countless other duties that had been his portion. At this present moment he wished he might have found their equivalent at the Abbey. If he could have chopped down trees or mended fences, he would have rejoiced at the labor. Though he had continued his cataloguing after Stephen Bardine had gone, the sensible conclusions he had formulated were being fast surmounted by his frustration. To have been so close to him and to have been forced to smile servilely and to speak mildly when he had ached to strike him down or strangle him or both had wrought upon his mind to the point where he was seething with rage. He glared about him at a chamber which had suddenly become much too small to contain him. Rain notwithstanding, he would have to go outside!

Striding to the door, he emerged into the hall and was at the front door when he was suddenly confronted by Miss Seton, her long, thin face full of anxiety. "Oh, dear Mr. Bidewell," she murmured. "She has not returned . . . and she would not take Thomas with her, though I thought she should . . . I pray she has not met with an accident. She should have been back ere now . . . she promised she would not be gone long. . . ."

Extracting the kernel from the shell of her conversation, he said, "Miss de Beaufre has gone out?"

"On Albion . . . he is sure-footed and she is an excellent horsewoman, but in this weather . . . I sent Thomas out to search for her an hour ago and he returned saying he could not find her . . . of course the rain would have quite obliterated Albion's tracks . . ." She sighed. "I do not know why I am telling you all this for you cannot help, being unfamiliar with the Park . . . there are so many byways . . . I really do not know what I can do and I am concerned . . . she will be soaked to the skin!"

"When did she leave?" he asked.

"Fully two hours since . . . and this downpour should have brought her back! I cannot imagine anything more unpleasant than riding in the rain. I have done so myself, being caught out on the way back from visiting a parishioner with my brother, and was wet through and only avoided a quinsy because of Mrs. Meager, our cook, who had acquired some remedies from her grandmother, which I cannot now remember . . . though poor Bryony would find them useful, I am sure . . ."

"Did she tell you that she had any particular destination in mind?" he interrupted.

"Mrs. Meager?" Miss Seton looked surprised. Then she flushed. "Oh, dear, I am not thinking clearly, am I? No, she only said she must ride. The child was a mite edgy. Sir Stephen . . . so importunate, you understand. Yet I expect that waiting such a long while to be wed has been . . . difficult. He is a young man of an ardent disposition and so much in love with her. Long engagements are so difficult. It was most unfortunate, Honoria dying . . . you know I had always thought her illnesses were less severe than she imagined, which shows how very much in error I was . . .Honoria was Bryony's mama . . . the relict of my third cousin Anthony . . . but that is aside from the point. I do hope Bryony comes back soon . . ."

"Perhaps if you might allow me to take one of the horses, I could search for her," he said.

Her eyes lighted. "Oh, could you! That would be a great help. But you are not familiar with the grounds, are you? It is a vast area and you, too, might become lost and in this weather . . ."

"I have covered quite a bit of it in my walks," he said carefully. "I cannot say for sure that I could be of any assistance, but I should be happy to make the effort."

"Well, I cannot see that it would hurt . . . though it is dreadfully wet outside."

"I am no stranger to bad weather," he told her.

"You are very kind. Oh, I cannot understand why she did not take Thomas with her. She ought to have done so . . . there is a lack of propriety in a young woman riding alone . . . though of course, the Park. I told her there was every indication that it would rain, too. My arm always aches . . . a fall you know . . . twenty winters since . . ."

"I will leave at once, Miss Seton," he said hastily.

The wooded reaches of the park, ghostly in the rain-blurred distance, filled Mr. Bidewell's mind with images of his past. As he urged Francesca, the chestnut mare Thomas had provided, along the muddy paths, it seemed to him that he could almost see the small, troubled, rotund figure that had been himself as a child, trudging before him, anxious to find a haven where he might be free of the gardener's boy, who jeered at him whenever he ventured into the grounds adjacent to the Court. Then that vision changed into the unhappy lad he had been at thirteen, grown taller but still heavy and unable to make friends with the slender, active sons of the neighboring gentry. In common with the gardener's boy, they had teased and ridiculed him; he had received much the same treatment from his tutor, Martin Blake. Mr. Blake had not scrupled to let him know he thought him an insensitive clod. Yet, Mr. Bidewell reasoned, that had been as much his fault as that of his tutor; for by then he was well on the way to developing the easygoing manner that served to mask his sensitive nature. How might Blake know what ardent fires burned behind his fleshy exterior? How could he understand that this gross youth dreamed of performing valorous deeds and rescuing distressed damsels? It was those dreams which had driven him to seek the solitude of the Park, and that he was trespassing had not disturbed him, since it had lessened the chances of his being discovered before he was ready to brave his lessons again.

During one of these forays he had encountered Bryony de Beaufre, who, of course, he knew, since they were related. He had been more annoyed than pleased on that meeting—for what might a man of thirteen have to do with a girl of seven—but, being by nature kindhearted, he had not driven her away. Then as her patent adoration had manifested itself, she had become very important to him for she alone had seemed to look upon him with uncritical eyes, evincing a respect for his greater wisdom that had been an entirely new experience for him. Yet it had not been until the following year that he could bring himself to share his greatest secret with her—the stone hut by the forest pool which he had called his "castle." It had seemed a castle, for it gave evidence of having been surrounded by a high wall and there were the remains of a small tower, too. However, when he had grown older he had found a book in his library detailing the history of De Beaufre Abbey, which had once sheltered a brotherhood of Carthusian monks. Some years before it had been built, one Sir Gladwin Woodhull, who had gone with King Richard to the Crusades and on returning from the Holy Land had, as an act of penance for some unknown but mortal sin, built himself a forest retreat, where he had lived out his days in prayer and fasting, gaining himself a reputation that bordered on saintliness. It had been his abstemious life that had inspired another equally sinful peer to turn monk and endow the Abbey, though in another more convenient section of the park.

Since Lucas had found a small stone cross not far from the ruined tower, he guessed that he had discovered Sir Gladwin's dwelling. Despite that knowledge, he and Bryony had continued to call it their castle. Beside the pool they had picnicked, and they had also maintained their animal hostel, sheltering their rescued creatures in its one large room.

He had visited it last just after he had returned from Brighton. He had sat near the pool, staring into it and seeing, on its dark green surface, the reflection of Bryony. There had been many other memories in that pool, which had been the more painful because he was positive that Lady Honoria would urge or even push Bryony into marriage, and that he must needs steel himself against the agony of losing the only woman who could ever mean anything to him.

Then—he winced at the recollection—he had returned to London and to the unwelcome realization that Bryony's regard for him had been less than he had imagined. Yet even then he could not have envisioned four years without the sight of her, any more than he could have known that in the course of those years there would be many women who would care for him—starting with the half-wild little Creole in New Orleans, after his release from prison. Marie her name had been and it was she who had introduced him to those pleasures about which he had only fantasized before. He had been weak and ill from his harsh treatment in the prison, and he had stayed with her for several months, gaining strength and some insight into the workings of the female mind. She had wept when he had left her and he, too, had had some regrets; but his desire for vengeance had made him restless. He had missed her a little, but other women had come to fill her place, eagerly and whether he willed it or not.

He frowned. He was not there to pride himself on all his easy conquests. Yet in a sense he was grateful to those experiences, for they had served to put Bryony in the proper perspective—not as one who was hopelessly beyond his reach, a goddess to be worshipped—but as a young woman he had loved once and for whom he still had a sentimental attachment but nothing more. He knew that now—because, having met Stephen Bardine again, all his incipient fondness for her had vanished, shriveled in the white fires of the hate that filled his soul to the exclusion of all other emotions. She was the betrothed of his enemy and as he had already determined, she must share in his downfall. Furthermore—his eyes gleamed—he had suddenly conceived a plan whereby that downfall might be effected. If he could not challenge Sir Stephen Bardine in his guise of Orion Bidewell, he could give him a reason to call him out—but that reason hinged on one circumstance—that Bryony might have taken refuge in the castle. Quite fervently he prayed to whatever power might heed him that she had. He was whistling as he urged Francesca onward for logic told him that there was no other place she might go.

SIX

Wind-driven rain splattered against Bryony's face and caused Albion to toss his head and emit one more in a series of snuffling snorts. "Easy, dear boy," she murmured, patting his neck. "We have arrived."

She slipped from her saddle, and led him to the elderly oak that grew hard by the remains of Sir Gladwin's modest efforts at tower construction. Tethering him to a branch and administering a conciliatory pat on his nose, she ran to the squat, stone structure she and Lucas had called their castle, and, keeping close to its wall in the vain hope that its small projecting rim of roof would keep some of the pelting rain off of her, she made her way to its narrow portal and cautiously peered inside. There was, she reasoned, always a chance that some manner of animal might have found its way inside. Once

Lucas had discovered a badger crouched in a corner, and another time a fox had sped out just as he had come in. However, a glance around the small, square room showed her that there was only an accumulation of dried leaves and dead branches, blown into it through its one window, set high in the right wall. As she entered it she shivered. It was cold and she looked longingly at the large hearth which Sir Gladwin had built against the center wall. However, even if she had had a tinderbox, it would have been impossible to start a fire. With a rueful little smile, she remembered Lucas's efforts in that direction. She could see him bringing in the logs and excitedly striking the flint only to discover that the flue was useless —which, they had agreed, as they had hastily fled the choking blue smoke, was not surprising after seven hundred years!

She moved to a corner and sat down, clutching her knees against her for warmth. Her pelisse habit was very damp and its cotton wadding had turned lumpy from the wetting she had received. Since she had elected not to wear its matching silk turban, her hair was also wet. It would probably dry soon, but she had no such hopes for her habit; and that was unfortunate, for it was possible she might have to spend the night here and, very likely, would have caught a cold before morning.

"I should have listened to Cousin Anne," she remarked out loud and was startled by the echo her voice raised in that empty and surprisingly high-ceilinged chamber. She had forgotten the echo. She had not been back to the castle since the disappearance of Lucas. She would not have sought it out this afternoon had not the rain driven her there. She had not even been sure she would be able to find it, but once she had come in what she had imagined to be its general direction, she had passed the lightning-blasted oak and seen the glimmering surface of the deep forest pool that stretched beside it. Then she had sighted the lichen-covered rock with the splash of orange paint on its side. Lucas had done that so that they could always see it—even on cloudy days and on this cloudy, rain-swept day, it had been plainly visible— even though the color was fainter now. After all, it had been nearly fourteen years since he had daubed the boulder. She had watched him and she could see him now, his big body crouched beside it, puffing a little as he did after any exertion, no matter how small.

Resolutely, she shut the eye of her mind. She did not want to see him—but in this room, it was impossible not to see, not to remember, not to speculate on what might have happened to him. Oddly enough, she was still not sure that he had died, at least not all the time. There were moments when she was reasonably certain of it, but others when she was equally positive that he might be alive. In her dreams, he was always living.

There was one particularly vivid and recurring dream that concerned the castle. In it, she would follow the markers and enter the glade, moving past the ruined wall and the broken tower. Then, on entering the hut, he would be waiting and chiding her because she had not come in such a long time. She would kneel beside him, saying earnestly, "But Lucas, I feared you were dead." And he would answer, "But I have been here all this while, Bree," and she would endeavor to explain why she had thought him dead and the explanations would be so difficult, so painful and he would not understand—just as he had not understood that day in the curricle, she knew he had not—and she had hoped that later she would be able to convince him that she had been only surprised at his show of strength, surprised and pleased, but there had been no later. She ran her hands through her hair, wishing she could brush away that memory—all memories from her mind—but if she did not dwell on Lucas, she must needs thinks of Stephen!

Her hand flew to her lips. She had hated his kiss—hated being caught in his hard embrace and forced to endure it. Cousin Anne had brought him to his senses that afternoon, but what would happen when she was his wife? No Cousin Anne would be on hand to interfere then. She would need to endure his hateful caresses and there would be much more with which to contend than mere kisses!

In spite of her strictures concerning what was proper for a single female to hear, Chrissie, out of long-established habit, had gleefully confided in Bryony, waxing extremely descriptive over the various joys of holy wedlock. Remembering them, Bryony shook her head and moaned, "I cannot . . . I cannot." Yet other than running away, which, in honor to her mother's memory, she could not do, she saw no alternative. In another month she would be forced to wed him, forced to suffer those intimacies that were the lot of a wife.

"You are so fortunate, Bryony!"—Chrissie again, rolling her dark, knowing eyes and saying appreciatively, "Sir Stephen is uncommonly handsome and there is no one more charming." Many other young women would have agreed with her—even Cousin Anne had often told her that she considered Sir Stephen a most attractive gentleman. She could admit his attraction. She did not dislike him, it was only that she did not love him. She wondered why, and knew that in the back of her mind there remained a small tendril of the distrust she had originally felt for him. Thinking on it, she realized that in the past few hours that distrust had increased. Certainly he had been most peremptory in his talk of closing the Abbey, quite as though it were his property. Then with a little jolt of shock, she realized that it soon *would* be—since when a woman married, her estate passed into her husband's keeping, unless otherwise stipulated in a father's will. Sir Anthony, dying before his daughter was of an age to be wed, had made no such provision. A feeling of helplessness swept over her and coupled with it was anger. She did not want Stephen to determine the fate of her old home; yet knowing him, she was sure that once they were married, he would insist upon returning to the Court. He loved the beautiful old mansion; how often she had heard him praise the fine pictures and the exquisite furnishings Lucas had bought for it. She loved them, too. She had been consulted as to the merit of several of his acquisitions. A tender little smile played about her lips. She was sure that he had sought her advice merely to flatter her—for his own taste could not be faulted. Tears squeezed forth from her eyes and rolled down her cheeks. She could not live there in Lucas's home with Stephen, whom she could not but consider an interloper! It would be a desecration!

"Oh, Lucas . . . Lucas . . ." she moaned, envisioning him now, in every corner of the room. "If you only knew how much I long for you!"

A gust of rain-laden wind blew in through the door and the dry leaves rattled as if beneath a sudden footfall. She remembered her thoughts concerning Lucas's ghost in the Abbey—how much more fitting if he had come to her here. "Perhaps you have come, Lucas," she murmured. "Perhaps you have heard me. I wish you had. If I cannot have you living, I should welcome your spirit." It seemed to her that the wind had died down and the room grown preternaturally silent. Then with a chill that

117

seemed to invade the very marrow of her bones, she heard the rattling of a harness and the neigh of a horse. Leaping to her feet, she ran to the doorway, peering out across the misty glade—had he come to her on his ghostly steed? She achieved a shaky laugh. Because of his girth, he had rarely ridden horses and that neigh had probably arisen from the throat of poor, drenched Albion. So much for ghosts! Judging from her reaction, she would not be as comfortable with Lucas's spectre as she had believed.

She tensed. Once more, the jingling of a harness smote her ears and coupled with it was the sound of hooves. Someone was nearing the entrance to the glade. Staring in that direction she saw a horseman, sitting tall in his saddle. With a gasp of fear, she moved away from the doorway, praying that he had not seen her. Stephen had warned her that the woods were full of poachers. "Some," he had said, "are boys from the village—others are ruffians who'd not scruple to rob or worse." He had not elaborated upon the "worse," but Mary had spoken of a village girl found murdered on the grounds of another estate in a way she had described as " 'orrid nasty."

The sound of the horse's hooves grew louder and then stopped. She longed to look out and see if he were still there, but she did not dare. If only she had gone out to Albion, then she could have ridden away. Perhaps she might yet make a run for it—but even as this thought rose in her mind, the entrance was blocked and invaded by a man she recognized at once. "Mr. Bidewell!" she exclaimed.

He started and stared at her in amazement. "Miss de Beaufre. What are you doing in this place?"

She got slowly to her feet. "I came here to escape the rain."

"By God!" He continued to stare at her. "I . . . I can scarce believe it. I had given up all hope of finding you."

"You were looking for me?"

"Miss Seton was distressed at your long absence; she feared you might have suffered a mishap." He added anxiously, "I pray you have not."

"No, as I explained, it began to rain quite hard and being too far away to return to the Abbey, I came to the castle."

"The . . . castle?" he repeated uncertainly.

She smiled, "It is what my Cousin Lucas and I used to call it when we were little. It was our secret place. . . ." She shook her head. "I cannot imagine how you happened upon it. No one ever has before, at least not while we were here. It is so very sequestered."

"I grant you that," he agreed. "I expect I came upon it because I myself was quite hopelessly lost. I have often walked through the Park. That is why I told Miss Seton that I might be able to find you, but what with the rain and the wind, poor Francesca grew confused and took me in an entirely different direction before I was quite aware of it and when I tried to turn back . . ." He shrugged and held out his hands in a hopeless gesture. "I am sure you can understand."

"I most certainly can," she smiled. "The Park is a natural maze."

He smiled. "Then how fortunate I was to find you instead of the Minotaur in its center." He glanced about him curiously. "Yes, this might be the very center of a labyrinth. I could hardly believe my eyes when I saw it. What is it? It looks to be of ancient origin."

"It dates back to the thirteenth century. Lucas said it was a hermit's cell—the man built it as part of his penance and lived here forty years."

"Forty years," he marveled. "I hope he was forgiven his sins. Certainly he deserved to be."

She scented ridicule in his tone and was immediately defensive. "We loved it, Lucas and I."

"I can well imagine that. It would be a great adventure for a child, finding so hidden a dwelling."

Her eyes grew a little misty. "It was . . . we had such good times here, Lucas and I. It was he who discovered it."

"Indeed? What was he like, this cousin of yours?"

"Lovely," she breathed. "My best friend in all the world."

"Best friends are not easy to find. It must have been hard indeed to lose him then," he said sympathetically.

"Very hard," she replied with a catch in her voice.

Striding to the doorway, he stared into the pelting rain. "I thought I should escort you home, but I do not see that we can leave yet."

"Oh, no, we must wait until the rain stops. I should have heeded my Cousin Anne and started back sooner. I saw the clouds massing but expected nothing more than an April shower."

"And instead, a veritable flood. I, too, was surprised at its force." He stared at her habit. "It would seem that you were drenched. I have a tinderbox. Should we not light a fire? I see a few branches have fallen in here . . . they are dry and would afford us some heat." He glanced at the hearth.

"No, we dare not," she said hastily. "The flue does not carry out the smoke."

"But you cannot be very warm," he frowned. "If my own coat were not soaked through, I should give it to you."

"Please, do not worry. I am well enough," she assured him. "But you should remove your jacket . . . it is very wet."

"I expect I should," he said hesitantly. "If you would not mind . . ."

"Mind!" she laughed. "Come, Mr. Bidewell. I am not such a stickler for the proprieties that I should want you to catch a chill. I only hope you'll not be too cold without it."

"I rarely feel the cold," he assured her. "Besides, we should not need to remain here long. The rain will no doubt be over soon. Usually the heavier the cloudburst, the quicker it expends itself.

Recalling her initial fears about the duration of that rain, she flushed. There was, she knew from past experience, more than a chance that they would be stranded there the whole of the night. "Possibly . . ." she began, meaning to explain that rather than a cloudburst it was a storm, she paused, deciding against imparting that particular bit of information. Given his innate courtesy, he might think it incumbent upon himself to leave her: and as far as she knew, there was no other spot he might shelter.

"You were about to say, Miss de Beaufre?" he prompted.

She achieved a blank stare. "Do you know," she returned with a slight laugh, "I have quite forgotten what I wanted to say." A trifle nervously, she continued, "Will you not sit down? You might be thinking the ground is damp, but it isn't here . . . away from that window. It's a little warmer on this side of the room. It is a pity we have no door to shut but . . ."

His laugh quelled her explanations. "I am not put off by the cold or the damp. Let me assure you, Miss de

Beaufre, that this cell is a veritable palace compared to some of the places I have stayed."

She raised startled eyes to his. "I am sorry for that."

"Sorry? Why should you be?"

"It suggests to me that you've not always been very comfortable."

Shrugging himself out of his jacket, he replied, "No, I have not always been very comfortable. Yet you need not be sorry for that. I have survived my hardships and in many ways, I am much the better for them."

She noted that his shirt, though clean, was much mended and by an inexpert needle which she guessed must be his own. The sight of those large, crooked stitches served to excite her pity the more. "I cannot believe that anyone is the better for hardships," she commented.

"Ah, but they are," he contradicted. Kneeling, he gathered some branches and brushing off the dust that had accumulated on them, he pushed them together and laid his discarded coat carefully across them. "All of us are prone to certain illusions which we are happier—or should I say safer—without." He had not been looking at her as he had spoken but now he faced her and she fancied that there was a sardonic gleam in his eyes.

"You believe it wrong to have illusions?" she asked curiously.

"Dangerous," he corrected.

"In what way?"

Rising, he stared at her intently. "When you put your faith in someone whom you really do not know."

"And . . . then you find them untrustworthy?" she asked.

"And then you find them untrustworthy," he replied.

She was silent a moment. "Yet," she said finally, "sometimes you know instinctively whom you can trust. For instance, I trust you, Mr. Bidewell."

He looked a little taken aback. Then frowning, he said almost harshly, "You do not know me, Miss de Beaufre."

"I do not know *about* you," she corrected.

"Is there a difference?"

She nodded. "We've had little opportunity to speak. I do not know where you were born or where you grew to manhood or what disappointments or reverses you may have suffered. However, I do know that you are both kind and honorable."

He stared at her, the frown still mirrored in his eyes. "You cannot know that," he said repressively.

"Let us say, Mr. Bidewell, that you may not have always acted honorably or kindly, but if you did not, I am convinced that it would have been by force of circumstances rather than by will. I feel that I am right."

He exhaled a long breath. "And I tell you, that one can rely too much upon intuition."

"Are you also telling me that I ought to be afraid of you?" she inquired with a slight smile. "I am not. I could not be, not after seeing you with that owl."

He laughed. "The owl?"

"Yes," she said positively. "And I feel quite as safe as that owl."

Meeting her beautiful, candid eyes, he said in a curiously muted tone, "You are right, Miss de Beaufre, you are quite as safe as that owl. But . . . you should not trust everybody."

"I do not trust everybody," she assured him.

"That is good to hear," he said in somewhat constricted tones. Glancing at the window, he grimaced. "The rain . . . I wish it might stop and I could bring you back to the Abbey."

She smiled. "Or it might be that I will have to lead you back, since you are a stranger here."

He laughed shortly. "True, I'd not thought of that."

"Either way—" she moved to the left of the hearth—"until we may go, come sit down."

"Upon the ground and tell sad stories of the death of kings?" he asked lightly.

"I wish you may, and other stories, too," she said with some eagerness. "You must know many, given all the libraries where you have worked . . . and all the books you've read."

The square of sky framed in the window of the castle had gone from pale grey to deep gunmetal, and the darkening room had become considerably colder. In the ensuing hours they had discussed numerous topics, from the late Sir Anthony's interest in literature and antiquities to the dress of the Choctaw Indians Mr. Bidewell had encountered in Louisiana. He had also heard and approved of Bryony's novel. An enthusiasm, unmarked by any trace of condescension, had fallen very sweetly on her ears and she had not hesitated to tell him so. But in the last thirty minutes conversation had faltered and become constrained, interrupted by periods of silence. Breaking one of these, she said self-consciously, "Gracious, the rain seems as heavy as ever. Fancy, last Monday, I had thought it would be a warm April!"

"The weather's always uncertain here . . . in all parts of England." He paused, then said tentatively, "I cannot think that it would be wise to try and return to the Abbey tonight."

"N-no," she agreed, "we dare not chance it. The paths must be sadly mired."

He cleared his throat. "Miss de Beaufre, I fear you will take a chill if you lie here all the night in this cold and damp. I can fix you a bed of leaves but . . . under the circumstances, it were better if we remained close to each other for . . . warmth. I am quite aware of the impropriety attendant upon my suggestion, but let me assure you . . ."

"You need give me no assurances, Mr. Bidewell," she said crisply. "If we are both to be warm, I can think of no other solution and it *has* become exceedingly raw."

"Exceedingly. It is a pity we may not have a fire or something warm to drink. Soup or even brandy. Since we do not, let us hope that sleep will come as soon as possible."

"I pray it will," she said, glad that she could sound equally detached when, actually, and in spite of her oft-reiterated statements concerning her trust in him, she was aware of various flutterings in chest and throat.

Yet amazingly enough, once he had piled up the leaves and instructed her to lie close against the wall, that incipient fear, if she might term it such, had vanished nor did it return, not even when he lay down beside her and pulled her against him. There was something quite impersonal in the way he held her and nothing could have been more respectful than the tone of voice in which he said, "Rest your head upon my shoulder, Miss de Beaufre. So. You will be more comfortable."

Though she complied, she was rather certain that she would enjoy little sleep that night. Still, once her ear was attuned to the steady beat of his heart, her eyelids began to feel amazingly weighted, and in a very short time she sank into a deep slumber. Consequently she was completely unaware of how very long it took Mr. Bidewell to follow that enviable example.

Years ago, the forest pool, deeply green and extending for some little distance into the wooded fastness of the glade, had intrigued the boy Lucas. His lively imagination had pictured it as abounding with strange fish and odd aquatic plants. He had longed to dive into its depths and explore its wonders at close range, but his all-abiding fear of water had kept him chained to its banks. He had never even ventured to follow Bryony's example and wade in its shallows. Now, resting against its farthermost end and further concealed by the overhanging branches of a weeping willow, he could laugh at his younger, timorous self. Poor fat little Lucas Bardine had never known the exhilaration of a swim through these icy waters. It was not only refreshing to the body but it cleared the mind, something he had sorely needed that morning.

He reddened, remembering his conflicting emotions upon awakening to find Bryony still slumbering in his embrace. He had seen many sleeping women, but none had appeared more desirable than the girl who had lain so trustingly in the circle of his arms. He clenched his teeth, remembering how difficult it had been to fall asleep the previous night. It had been twenty times more difficult to refrain from kissing her into wakefulness. He had not expected to be so aroused by one who was, after all, no more than a cog in the mechanism of his revenge again Stephen Bardine.

As he had told himself repeatedly, before and during his days in Miss de Beaufre's library, he had totally recovered from his youthful adoration for her. Yet after all, he was a man, and of a nature warm and passionate. It was not easy to lie in such close proximity to a beautiful woman without longing to possess her. The water about him rippled from his sudden impatient movement. If he were to be totally honest with himself, he must admit that it was more complicated than that. It was the realization of a dream that had often troubled the sleep of the gross, unhappy boy he had been. With a twinge of pain, he recalled his desperate longing to be more than the friend she now described with such affection. She had always been affectionate, but he had always wanted more than her affection; and last night, in a sense, that most exciting of youthful fancies had been realized. He had actually lain in the castle with Bryony in his arms. His mouth twisted and he bit down a short laugh. If he were to be absolutely specific, he had lain there clutching the woman engaged to marry his wicked cousin. It was important that he keep that in mind—important, too, that he remember the reason why he had come there. It had nothing to do with old fancies. Rather, it was specifically based on his memories of other rainy days, when two children had sought shelter in that particular sanctuary. He had been almost positive that he would find her there. Well, he had not been disappointed; and as he had expected, the rain had increased in intensity, forcing them to remain throughout the night. Furthermore, she had not, as he had feared, raised any objections. Indeed, she had been singularly tractable—this, despite his words concerning trust. He frowned, wondering what had prompted him to offer them. Stephen had been in his mind, but he might almost have been warning her against himself. However, she had not been warned. Again the water rippled about him, as he recalled her staunch assertions concerning her conclusions as to his own character. His smile was very close to a sneer. Once he had been the man she described—honorable and . . . stupid. Kind, because he had never been given any reason why he had not to be. It was different now—just as his body had changed, and that he could not regret, so had his soul. It would never have occurred to the honorable Lucas Bardine that his adored Bryony might be used as a device to ensnare his Cousin Stephen.

"Bait," he murmured, "that is all she is." A contemptuous smile lifted the corner of his lip. Given Stephen's jealous and possessive nature, he was positive that once Stephen learned of Bryony's night in the woods, nothing would keep him from forcing a duel on Mr. Bidewell, the librarian—and learn of it he would. Servants talked and they mingled with other servants. None knew that better than he, who, in addition to taking some of his meals in the kitchens of the Abbey, had found refuge in other kitchens during his days in America. The news of Bryony de Beaufre's misadventures would spread like wildfire and must soon reach the master of Bardine Court. Then he frowned. Unbidden, a vision had risen before his eyes—Bryony, lying against him, her gold-shot curls tousled about her face, her dark lashes sweeping her pale cheeks, a faint smile upon her parted lips . . .

"So lovely . . . so lovely," he muttered. So lovely and so trusting, as well . . . and innocent. His frown deepened. If it were known that she had been with him in the woods, no one would believe her innocent. Her reputation would be ruined, her name besmirched. She would be ostracized and . . . but that did not matter! What mattered was Stephen, Stephen, Stephen! He sank beneath the surface of the pool. In its depths grew plants with long feathery leaves, tangled masses of them, brushing his bare skin. If Stephen had had his way, his drowned body would have lain in deeper waters, caught among the seaweed. He shot to the surface, spitting out a mouthful of the water and draining it from his ears. He glanced down at his marred chest. Only Stephen's blood would atone for those pictures! Bryony was no longer his concern!

"Liar," he muttered bitterly. She had been the friend of Lucas Bardine—was still his friend. In the name of Lucas Bardine, he could not betray her. It had all been for naught—all his carefully laid plans. If he had really thought about it, he would have known that from the beginning, but he had acted impulsively, on the spur of the moment. He kicked away from the bank and swam across the pool to where Francesca was placidly cropping grass; he was moved to fling himself upon her back and ride away, but he could not do that, either. He swam to the willow tree and addressed himself to this new problem.

The fact of their night together remained—but if they were to return to the Abbey at different times and from different directions, the gossips could make nothing of that. Fortunately, no one knew of the castle. He smiled ruefully. A little earlier that morning, he'd been willing that everyone should know of it. Absently, he stared at the red V on his left arm. His vengeance must be cut from other cloth.

His plans concerning their return to the Abbey were on the tip of his tongue when he came to the castle door. Pausing, he called tentatively, "Miss de Beaufre . . . might I come in?"

There was no answer. She might yet be sleeping, he

thought, but on peering inside, he found the room empty. Seized by a sudden suspicion, he went around to the spot where he had seen her horse tethered the night before. He was not surprised to find it gone. He laughed. In formulating and rejecting his schemes, he had given scant thought to Miss de Beaufre's state of mind. As a child, he now recalled that she had been extremely resourceful. Obviously, she had not changed. As on many other occasions, she had taken matters into her own capable little hands.

"Good morning."

He whirled to find her standing behind him and his own greeting trembled to silence on his lips. She was looking even more beautiful than she had when he awakened. Her hair, released from its pins and combs, rippled down her back, and with her pale skin, her large glowing eyes, and her clinging green habit, she resembled a forest fay —Titania, perhaps. Again he was annoyed at thoughts which were far more suited to the poetic soul of the dreaming Lucas Bardine than to the purposeful man he had become. "Good morning, Miss de Beaufre," he said with a slight bow.

"Your hair is wet," she observed. "Have you been swimming, then?"

He nodded. "I thought I should get back before you awakened. I hope you were not alarmed to find me gone."

She flushed slightly. "Oh, no, I saw Francesca by the pool." She sighed. "I have been looking for Albion. I fear I did not tie him securely enough last night. I pray he went back to the stables."

"Good God," he exclaimed, "has he gone!"

To his surprise, she appeared singularly undisturbed

by the mishap, merely commenting, "I hope Francesca will bear the two of us."

"But . . ." he began, frowning as the irony of the situation smote him. If he had still been minded to put his scheme into operation, the disappearance of Albion would have been singularly fortuitous. As it was . . .

"I expect," she observed, "that if we were to be seen coming back together, I should be hopelessly compromised."

He hesitated and then, resolutely, he put temptation aside and said, "We must not be seen together. I can take you part of the way . . . then, you must continue by yourself . . . on foot. You can explain that Albion fell. I am sure you could affect a limp . . . I shall return later and explain I could not find you." He gave her a reassuring smile. "I think Miss Seton will believe me since, after all, I am a stranger to these parts."

She gave him a long look. "That does seem a most ingenious explanation." She glanced away quickly and it seemed to him that her cheeks had grown pinker. "I . . . I slept very well last night, Mr. Bidewell. You were most . . . considerate. I felt almost as though I were with my Cousin Lucas."

He turned cold. "Indeed?" he said through stiff lips. "Do I remind you of him in some way?"

"Not in the least. It's only that I always felt so protected when I was with him. I felt that same protection last night. I do thank you for that."

He went limp with relief. "You've no need to thank me. Any gentleman—"

"I am not in agreement with you," she interrupted. "I have the feeling that few gentlemen would have been so considerate." Moving closer to him, she fastened her eyes on his face. Then after a moment of silence, she said hesitantly, "I am in a most unfortunate situation. . . ." She paused and a brighter color stained her cheeks. "But first . . . I must ask you. Are your affections fixed upon some female? Are you betrothed or even married, Mr. Bidewell?"

"No, I am not," he answered, looking at her in some surprise.

Her eyes flickered away from his face and fastened on her boot. "About my situation . . . I think you know that I am betrothed to Sir Stephen Bardine?"

"I know that," he answered, thinking that he now understood her reasoning. If he had been married, the poor child might have believed herself safe. Ironically, it was up to him to reassure her. "No doubt you are worried about repercussions. He need never know. If we do as I suggested—"

"Mr. Bidewell," she broke in almost curtly, *"I want him to know."* Meeting his astonished gaze, she continued diffidently, "You see . . . the agreement between us was not of my choosing. My Mama was uncommonly taken with Sir Stephen. On her deathbed which he, too, attended, she . . . she bade us join hands and in what was practically her dying breath, she made me promise that I should wed him. Though. . . my affections were otherwise engaged, I could not refuse. And now . . . the period of mourning is nearly at an end. Next month he expects to post the banns."

His head was whirling. It seemed to him that he should have guessed that Bryony could not have loved Sir Stephen, but she had said her affections were "otherwise engaged." Who, then, had she loved? He said tentatively, "It seems very unkind of your mother to have exacted

132

such a promise, if she knew you'd given your heart into another's keeping. Was this man so unacceptable?"

Her eyes were suddenly dark with sorrow. "He is dead. But I'd not talk of that. I have something very . . . unusual to propose. No doubt, you'll not even consider it, but I pray you'll think on it first."

She had become exceedingly agitated, he thought. Giving her a soothing smile, he said gravely, "I promise certainly that I shall think upon it."

She had taken a leaf from a nearby tree and she twirled it in her hand as she said haltingly, "If . . . if Sir Stephen were to . . . to find out that I was c—compromised, he might cry off . . . but again, he might not. I have a notion that he covets my dowry, which is large."

"Surely," he said harshly, "he is not without resources!"

"No, certainly not," she agreed. "He has inherited all that should have come to my Cousin Lucas. But he was once very poor and that, I think, has rendered him greedy. There is no need to discuss that now. It is only that I have the impression that he wants as much as he can acquire. Furthermore, our estates are adjoining and upon marrying me, he would assume control of both. However, if . . ." She hesitated again and swallowed nervously, then speaking rapidly, said, "If I were wed, he could do nothing. Mr. Bidewell, without meaning to . . . you have compromised me. I have heard of similar situations and often the gentleman has offered for the lady in question. If . . . because you are a gentleman, you might feel it your duty to protect me from scandal by . . . by offering for me, I should not refuse you. It would be a marriage in name only, of course. I should want nothing

133

else. However . . . if . . . if you were discreet, it would not need to interfere with your freedom . . . I know you are not wealthy . . . I could arrange that you had funds at your disposal. You would need to remain with me at the Abbey or at my house in town, but I would expect no other concessions from you . . . only that you would stay with me. But if in the future . . . you found the arrangement not to . . . to your liking, then . . . I expect the agreement could be annulled . . . but for the nonce, I should be most grateful if . . . if you would help me." She expelled a deep breath and, after one beseeching glance, looked away.

He opened his mouth and closed it, hardly trusting himself to speak, lest his exultation be apparent in his tone. Finally he said, "Miss de Beaufre, have you . . . have you given this arrangement real thought?"

She looked at him then. "Oh, yes I have," she said earnestly. "I . . . I know it must seem very strange to you, and very bold and . . . and most unmaidenly, as well. But . . . you see . . . I do trust you and surely Mama would agree that I had no alternative. She had a perfect horror of scandal!" Tears stood in her eyes. "Oh, Mr. Bidewell, I cannot . . . I will not wed Sir Stephen Bardine. There is something about him that frightens me. Please help me. You are my one hope." She flushed and moved away from him. "I can see you think me mad. I expect I am. I expect you cannot even consider—"

"Miss de Beaufre," he broke in, "if you are as truly determined on this course as you seem, I have some few stipulations . . . and if you agree to them I shall be glad to aid you in whatever way I may."

Her eyes brightened, "You would wed me, then? Oh, I did not dare hope . . ." She paused, adding a little uncertainly, "But you mentioned . . . stipulations. What might they be?"

"As you have said, I am not wealthy—" he began.

"I shall give you all my dowry!" she cried.

"I do not want it," he said harshly. "These are my stipulations. I want neither your dowry nor your estate. I want you to look upon this as a business transaction, as I shall myself. And as such, I want you to consider me still in your employ. I only ask that you pay me a salary commensurate with my supposed station. I think that as your husband, I must have more than one suit of clothing. Other than that, I want nothing from you and I should not ask that much were I not temporarily embarrassed. Meanwhile, I should like to continue in my capacity as your librarian and help you in any other way I may to earn this money."

"But . . . but I have said that I would give you—"

"I have heard what you have said, and you have heard my answer," he interrupted. "Is it agreeable to you?"

"I find it very strange . . . and generous, too. You are quite . . . quite unique, Mr. Bidewell and yes, it is agreeable," she whispered.

"Then," he smiled, "my dear Miss de Beaufre, will you do me the honor of becoming my wife?"

She stretched out her hands and as he grasped them, she said joyfully, "Oh, thank you, thank you, dear Mr. Bidewell. Yes, I shall be most happy to be your wife."

SEVEN

A dense fog, obscuring the gaslights that shone at intervals along London's streets, halted traffic on the main thoroughfares, causing a deal of cursing from the cabmen and those who drove the coaches and post-chaises of the Quality. Pedestrians were inclined to huddle together in protective clusters as they crossed the streets. There was always the chance that a curricle might sweep around the corner without notice and with serious consequences.

In the tortuous byways of Covent Garden the fog, impregnated here with the smell of rotting vegetables and fruits, was more welcome. Thieves plied their trade in its enshrouding obscurity, darting into misty corners and disappearing like ghosts. One such youth, an undernourished lad with a skin almost as grey as the fog, lank black hair straggling about a narrow face, and clad in garments so old and ragged that their shape was all but gone, slunk from doorway to doorway, his feral eyes intent on his quarry, who strode a few lengths in front of him. The boy's slit of a mouth was slightly parted and a drop of spittle gleamed on his chin; he was actually drooling in anticipation. The man was tall and handsome, a real swell in a many-caped coat, hanging open over a fine claret-colored jacket, brocade waistcoat and tight grey trousers strapped beneath highly-polished black boots. His shirt was ruffled, his cravat silk, the buttons of his coat brass, and, wonder of wonders, he had dared to sport gold fobs—all of which convinced the thief that he was queer in his noggin. It also meant that he must be carrying a fat purse full of the ready. It was not often such a rich bird fluttered into this particular basket. And before he flew out again . . . Then his eyes narrowed in disappointment and with some difficulty he choked down a cry of rage. Just as they were nearing the turn when he could have jumped him, the man suddenly veered off and went into Mabe's gin shop and before he came out, he would have been nimmed good and proper, damn his eyes! Spewing out a stream of oaths, which did nothing to relieve his fury, the thief sat down in a doorway and began to cry.

The gentleman, who had been quite aware of his follower and fully cognizant of the lad's frustration, smiled, then frowned. He had known similar disappointments as a youth, spent in this foul hole. He, too, had done his share of thieving, pimping and anything else that fell his way after his father had died of the "Blue Ruin" and his mother was well on the way to following his example. If it had not been for the actress who had been attracted by his handsome face and who had taught

138

him to speak like a gentleman and improve his natural assets, he might have been thieving yet, instead of presiding over Bardine Court, a landed Baronet, who would soon lay claim to De Beaufre Abbey, not to mention its lovely owner. He smiled, anticipating a time when that interfering old hag, Miss Seton, would not be able to send him packing. Indeed, it would be the other way around, and she back in her brother's vicarage, where she belonged, damn her. It had all worked out so beautifully. Lady Honoria had conveniently died but not before she had obliged him by deeding him her daughter. Bryony de Beaufre was quite the most luxurious of all the possessions he had coveted and eventually annexed from that bloated simpleton, who had gorged himself like the fat swine he so closely resembled, all those years while he had been starving on these same streets.

He scowled. If Lucas had come back . . . but it was not possible. The last they had heard was when the *Eagle* had sunk on Lake Borgne and given his utter terror of water, communicated to Mr. Platt his nephew and by Seaman Briggs, who had not only been instrumental in getting him aboard but who had actually wormed himself into his good graces—stupid, trusting Lucas!—he could not have survived. He smiled, recalling Briggs's letter concerning a flogging administered to Lucas in gruesome detail. The missive had been badly spelled but still it had described the episode very colorfully. He had to be dead, else he would have showed up before now. As he strode into the shop he saw Mabe and turned a grimace into another smile. The proprietor was seated with his uncle and a small, blonde girl in a tawdry gown. He was a lean, long-limbed man with watery blue eyes sunk deep in yellowish pouches; his skin was deeply scored with smallpox pits; clad in a dirty shirt and an equally dirty apron over battered trousers, he looked, Stephen thought disdainfully, even uglier than he had all those years ago, when a ragged little Stevie had timidly begged a pint of ale so that his mama could refresh herself between clients in the fetid rooms upstairs. His smile turned ironic as he met Mabe's envious glance. Then he strode to the table and stared at the girl. Close up she seemed little more than a child but, of course, her eyes gave the lie to that, being wise and hard beyond her years. As she sized him up they turned bright and glowing, while a practiced and inviting smile played about her lips.

He had no answering smile for her. "You'd be Nance?" he demanded coldly.

She appeared startled by the use of her name. "Y— Yes, sir," she assented.

"I been askin' 'er if she seen this 'ere seafarin' cove wot was askin' for me," his uncle informed him. "Seems as if she don't remember any such."

Stephen regarded her in silence and thought he discerned a look in her eyes which gave the lie to his uncle's statement. "This man would have been tall . . . and possibly heavyset."

"Briggs wrote as 'ow 'e'd dropped a lot o' that," his uncle reminded him. "Couldn't drop the tattoos, though. I told 'er about them."

"If you could remember such a man," Stephen continued, "it might be greatly to your profit."

"Profit?" she questioned.

"A guinea . . . two guineas."

"Two guineas?" She ran the tip of a small tongue around her lips, almost as though she could taste the words. "I . . . I seen lots o' men wi' tattoos," she said hesitantly and, it seemed to Stephen, almost reluctantly.

140

Mabe nudged her. "But this 'ere cove might've been different. 'E might've been the one wot spoke like a swell. You ain't forgotten 'im, 'ave you, Nance?"

"I've 'ad them, too," she said, giving Sir Stephen a provocative glance.

"But you was struck by this one," Mabe prompted. "Tol' me so. Said as 'ow 'e were different from the rest . . . said as 'ow 'e'd 'ad an 'ard time, an' been cut up by the cat'n you felt sorry for 'im."

"Cut up by the cat!" Oliver Platt's eyes narrowed and he exchanged a glance with Stephen. "Now that's real interestin'."

"Very," Stephen agreed grimly.

Nance regarded the pair of them warily and again, she licked her lips. Mabe was frowning at her and she knew he expected a share of the money and might cut up rough if he didn't get it. She said, "Ooooh, yes, now I remember. 'E were different an' talked the way you say. 'E treated me good."

"Was he tattooed?" Stephen questioned.

"Ooooh, yes, all over. 'Ad a big anchor on one arm'n a ship crost 'is chest." She paused, not liking the light that had flared into Stephen's eyes. It reminded her of a tabby at a mousehold, watchful and cruel. She added, " 'E 'ad a mermaid on 'is other arm."

"A mermaid!" Mr Platt exclaimed. "That wasn't me 'andiwork!"

"No matter," Stephen said. "Perhaps someone on board the *Eagle* had a sense of humor."

"That could've been," Mr. Platt agreed. "Briggs said as 'ow they 'ad a lot o' sport wi' 'im. An'——"

"Never mind that," Stephen interrupted impatiently. Turning back to the girl, he asked, "Did he tell you his name?"

141

She shook her head, "No, 'e didn't."

"Did 'e say why 'e was lookin' for me?" Mr. Platt demanded.

"Didn't tell me 'e was lookin' for you."

"Do you know where he went?" Stephen asked.

"That I do," she said.

"Where?" He caught her wrist, grasping it tightly, "Where did he say he was going?"

"Ooooh, you're 'urtin' me," she whined.

"Sorry." He dropped her wrist. "Where did he say he was going."

Rubbing her wrist, she said, "Told me as 'ow 'e were bound for Rio. Said as 'ow 'e didn't like London nor England neither . . . said as 'ow it were too cold'n 'e talked a lot about a . . . a Senorita, 'e called 'er . . . wot 'e left in Rio . . . said as 'ow we looked somethin' alike for all I 'ad blonde 'air . . . said 'e was goin' out on the *Sally-O*."

"I 'eard talk o' that," Mabe put in. "It's a merchant-man."

"That's right," Nance nodded. " 'E come in on a merchantman, too." She held out her hand. "Do I get my guineas?"

Sir Stephen grasped her by the shoulders staring into her eyes. "Are you telling me the truth, girl?" he demanded harshly.

"I swear I am," she gasped. "You're 'urtin' me. Lemme go!"

He released her so suddenly that she lost her balance and fell against the table. "Here." He dropped a pair of coins beside her. "Come, Oliver," he ordered and wheeled out of the shop.

Nance, clutching the money, got to her feet. Meeting Mabe's hard glance, she reluctantly handed him one of

142

the coins. Then she shivered. If that nice gentleman whose kindness she still remembered had run up against this cove and that other one, he must have fared badly. She smiled to herself, glad that she had had the forethought to lie.

"Well," Mr. Platt grinned, as they emerged onto the street. "Guess 'e's down wi' Davy Jones after all."

"Yes," Stephen agreed.

"Wot'll ye do now?" his Uncle inquired.

"Post the banns," Stephen smiled.

"Ain't it a little early?"

"I will do it as soon as I return from Paris," Stephen winked and his laughter, accompanied by that of Mr. Platt, raised a series of joyful echoes on that foggy street.

It was an April day such as the poets were wont to extol. The sky was an almost translucent blue and the sun, sliding down from its zenith, shed a golden glow over the hedgerows and gilded the budding trees. However, Miss Anne Seton, holding a handkerchief alternately to nose and eyes looked upon it with a feeling close to blame. Though fully aware that one cannot attribute human frailties to the climate, she could not help but think that if such fine weather had prevailed on the afternoon of the day before yesterday, when Bryony had gone on her ill-fated ride, they would not now be embarked upon an even more ominous journey, to the parish of the gentleman she was used to referring to as "my brother, the Vicar of Ardmore."

She could imagine that Hyperion would be very reluctant to perform the duty so soon to be thrust upon him, he, having known dear little Bryony since her cradledays. Yet, she was only too aware that since dearest

Felicity, his helpmate, was for the sixth time in a "delicate condition," he was in need of every penny that came his way. She darted a look at Bryony, sitting beside her in her white gown, which, while not absolutely bridal in appearance and fully three seasons old, being one of her London ensembles, yet it was muslin and trimmed with lace and far more festive in appearance than the half-mourning she had been wearing for the past eleven months. Considering the circumstances, she would have been better advised to wear black! Miss Seton sniffed and gulped and sniffed again. She glanced out of the window and, seeing Mr. Bidewell mounted on Francesca, the very horse he had ridden that fateful day, was shaken by a tremor. The idea of Bryony, who had been an Incomparable, and who might have married a Duke or Earl had she not fallen into what had amounted to a decline for no good reason that poor Honoria had ever been able to understand, was now being forced to throw herself away on a man without title or wealth was more than Miss Anne Seton could bear. However, there was nothing anyone could do about it. She had been out all night with Mr. Bidewell, a fact known by the staff at the Abbey, who must surely have communicated that information to everyone who would listen—for though the maids had been sternly enjoined not to breathe a word of it, she had guessed from their cast-down eyes and chancy glances that that word had long since taken wing. She could almost envision it in the form, say, of a bee, flitting from flower to flower—the flowers being the backstairs and servants' halls of country mansions throughout the length and breadth of Shropshire! Though Bryony had not socialized much since her mother had died, she was on good terms with the landed gentry whose estates lay along the Severn, and now . . . Miss Seton shuddered.

In that sense, one could only be glad that Mr. Bidewell had acted the gentleman and stood ready to give her his name, for once poor Sir Stephen was apprised of the facts—of Bryony sitting before Mr. Bidewell on Francesca, being brought back to the Abbey in the morning, well in view of those stablehands who knew that two stalls had remained empty during the night and that Albion had come back alone. It did not matter that Bryony had assured Mary that Mr. Bidewell had been the soul of honor. By the time the tale was communicated to the staff at the Court, it would have been much embroidered, and that was how it would reach Sir Stephen's ears. She released a quavering sigh. Poor, poor young man. His heart would be broken. Yet considering his devotion, he might have . . . Miss Seton quickly shook her head. No! He would have washed his hands of her—for what gentleman would be willing to take as his bride one who had lost her reputation and might be considered an abandoned woman! She sniffed again.

Bryony, viewing Miss Seton's lachrymose contenance, said sharply, "One would think we were going to a funeral, Cousin Anne."

Miss Seton, removing her handkerchief from her red-tipped nose, said lugubriously, "But is it not the death of all his hopes? I refer to poor Sir Stephen?"

Bryony firmed her lips. "It is marvelous to me, the spell that Sir Stephen manages to cast over most females, with only myself excepted."

"My dear, were you so reluctant to wed him, surely you might have told him so, long ago," Miss Seton pointed out.

"You know full well I was bound to it by my mother," Bryony retorted. "I should have stood by that promise . . . but Fate has decreed otherwise."

145

Miss Seton drew a deep breath and as she had several times yesterday and twice this morning, reiterated, "You know nothing about this man."

"I have told you that I do know something about him . . . and if it comes to that, I know very little about Stephen, either."

Miss Seton had the feeling that Bryony had suddenly gone daft. "He is your second cousin and the eighth Baronet of Bardine Court!" she exclaimed.

"Five years ago I was ignorant of his very existence and my Cousin Lucas stood ready to inherit the title that . . . that should have been his," Bryony retorted with fire in her eyes. "And were it not for his kindness and generosity, that nobody would not be sitting in his shoes!"

"I do not believe that one usually sits in shoes, my dear," Miss Seton said mildly.

"You know full well what I mean!"

"It was not Sir Stephen's fault that Lucas died," Miss Seton reminded her gently. "Oh, dear, I do not know what Hyperion is going to say."

"I am in hopes that it will be the marriage service!"

"That is a remark that smacks of levity!" Miss Seton reproved. "Oh, Bryony . . . if only you had not found it necessary to come back through High Town . . . at least the scandal could have been more confined . . ."

"We had hoped no one in the town would be astir so early. We could not come through the forest, the paths were too muddy. No one knows we sheltered in that little hut that Mr. Bidewell found . . ."

"The fact that you were together . . . ah, well, there is no need to dwell any longer upon the subject. What's done cannot be undone, but poor Sir Stephen . . . I shudder to think how he will receive this news. I wonder where he may be? Sally says he left early on the afternoon of the storm and that he seemed to be in a tearing rage."

"Sally seems marvelously well informed," Bryony commented sarcastically.

"I expect she met one of the servants from the Court. They always know ... oh, dear, oh, dear."

Bryony turned from Miss Seton with the suggestion of a flounce and stared out the window. Her annoyance vanished as she saw Mr. Bidewell. How well he looked astride Francesca. She smiled as she thought of their ride back to the Abbey. They had deliberately gone by way of the town and, as luck would have it, one Miss Paddock, who operated a circulating library and had the reputation of being a notorious gossip, had seen them. Bryony giggled, remembering the look on her face as she had taken note of their disheveled appearance at that early hour in the morning. Undoubtedly, it would take her a long time to live down the rumors that Miss Paddock would have started, but she did not care. She was free of Sir Stephen Bardine and, unlike Miss Seton, she had no fear of having fallen into an infinitely worse situation. There were concrete reasons for her belief but there was also her instinctive liking for the man. He was so obviously a gentleman. That had been apparent even without the account of his early life, given her as they had ridden home. He had had a hard time, poor man. A father who was a younger son and forced to earn his livelihood as a tutor and a mother, dying early. Younger sons were often treated abominably, as witness Stephen's father; except, of course, he had disgraced the family. She was sure that Mr. Bidewell's parent had never been guilty of such an indiscretion. Even though he had mentioned his mother only briefly, it was apparent that he came of gentle blood on both sides. She thought of how considerate he had been on the night of the storm and was immediately aware of odd pulses surging through her body. It had been such a wonderfully comfortable feeling—lying close against him and hearing the steady beat of his heart. She . . . Her thoughts had fled as he suddenly turned toward her and their eyes met. His face had been grave, but now he gave her a reassuring smile. Her regard for him increased and increased yet again as her gaze dropped to her reticule wherein reposed a special license and the agreement, witnessed by a shocked and weeping Cousin Anne, who should have approved, considering the fact that he had renounced all claim to her estates and dowry, accepting only the stipulated remuneration that he had mentioned before.

"Remuneration!" Cousin Anne had sobbed, "it is all so . . . so businesslike and unnatural!"

Bryony had rejoiced in his answer. He had said, "No more unnatural than that I should claim my wife's property for the return of my name. I am not a fortune hunter, Miss Seton."

Later, Miss Seton had seriously annoyed Bryony by remarking that Mr. Bidewell might be more devious than she thought, and what had appeared to be a noble renunciation could, in fact, be a clever ploy, and that he might take advantage of his situation in ways she could never envision!

She did not credit Miss Seton's raven-like croakings for one single instant. Reaching into her reticule, she patted those two documents which, in effect, spelled her freedom from nearly a year of bondage. Then without her willing it, Lucas was once more in her mind. It was odd how very often she thought of him in conjunction with Mr. Bidewell. As she had already noted, they did have something in common—they were both kind, both honest and, with a slight shock, she realized that had Lucas been slender, he might even have resembled Mr. Bidewell. They had similar coloring and they were about the same height, though she thought Lucas might have been shorter . . . or he might have only seemed shorter by reason of his bulk. As she gazed at Mr. Bidewell's slender but muscular frame, she smiled. A vision of the man, his hair wet from his swim in the pool Lucas had eyed with such terror, dispelled that comparison. It occurred to her that had Lucas suffered the hardships endured by Mr. Bidewell, he might have been the better for it. There was no doubt but that he had been shockingly overindulged and cosseted. That was why, in the years she had known him, she had never been able to consider him as more than her best friend. It was only after his disappearance that she had known that his other characteristics far surpassed his physical appearance. It was only then that she had known to her sorrow that she had lost far more than a mere friend. Yet now, much to her amazement, it seemed to her that the image of her adored Lucas, contrasted against the vibrant reality of Orion Bidewell, was growing considerably fainter.

"I still say that you know nothing about him!" Miss Seton exclaimed, with startling effect—for one pregnant moment, Bryony thought she had read her mind. Miss Seton continued, "He might have been a convict in New South Wales. Look at his hands! They are certainly not the hands of a gentleman!"

"They are the hands of a gentleman who, having fallen upon hard times, has been forced to work at any task he could find no matter now menial. His hands are well-shaped. Furthermore, I gave you his background."

"You have only his word on it and none to vouch for him! You cannot be sure he is telling you the truth! Why

I can think of a female in my brother's parish, who was beguiled by a stranger, such as Mr. Bidewell, well-spoken, very pleasant and, after she wed him, it was learned that he was a tinker's son! He made her life a misery and in the end he vanished with her jewels and the hall clock! You might not think that a clock was much of a loss, but this one was very old and . . ."

"Cousin Anne," Bryony said impatiently, "I do not think that Mr. Bidewell has any designs on our clocks, and furthermore I do not care what he has been. I know only that I . . . I . . ." Bryony's hand flew to her mouth as she realized what she had been about to say, but that was nonsense! She did not, could not love him! Even if she did not agree with Cousin Anne regarding his possible antecedents, he was a stranger. She must keep in mind that he was only doing her a favor. Undoubtedly he had no more than a friendly feeling for her. It behooved her to remember that and to be sensible. Glancing out of the window again, she met his eyes and, as he gave her another reassuring smile, she nodded, trying to keep her own gaze as impersonal as his.

The Parish Church of St. John in Ardmore was small and much to the chagrin of its Vicar, dated back to that period of church building, just after the Black Plague had devastated the land, which meant that rather than being in the beautiful architectural style known as the Decorated it was an example of the Perpendicular; its windows were uncompromisingly square, its doors had no more than a flattened arch, and its buttresses, parapets, pulpits, and fonds were covered with the most stereotyped sort of paneling. Its ornament work was depressingly square and stylized. Inded, the whole building had a depressed appearance, suggesting that those who had a hand in its construction were less than enthusiastic. Furthermore, though it had once been known for two very beautiful stained glass windows, these had been smashed by the Puritans and those that replaced them were no more than ordinary. The tower of the church had been beautiful but it had not survived the buffetings of time. This the Vicar bitterly attributed to inferior materials and a mayor who had pocketed much of the monies that should have been employed in its construction. Consequently, in the middle of the last century it had fallen, to be replaced by one which was merely commonplace, due to the indifference of a parsimonious town council.

However, in the twilight hour with the failing light diffused through its mullioned windows, bathing its interior in a soft orange glow, the effect was lovely. If a disinterested stranger had been present, he might have thought the young couple standing before the Vicar singularly fortunate in their choice of time, for they must certainly take with them a memory which might last them through the whole of a long and happy married life.

The Vicar was cognizant of that mellow glow, but it only served to depress him, rendering a countenance very similar to that of his sister—extremely melancholy. In common with that same sister, he had been markedly distressed by the circumstances attendant upon the wedding and, in consequence, highly reluctant to officiate. However, as Miss Seton had anticipated, the emolument had been too tempting for him to refuse Still, even as he stood before the altar, mentally consigning the money to a dozen needful places, not the least of these being the dry rot in the chancel, he hoped that when he reached that portion of the text when he must ask any person who knew of a just cause why these two should not be joined in Holy Matrimony, would he speak out or forever hold his peace, he would receive a show of hands or at least a hand. But, the announcement being greeted only by silence, he resolutely joined Miss Bryony Constance Honoria Verity de Beaufre, spinster, to Mr. Orion Bidewell bachelor, according to the powers vested within himself resignedly and lugubriously pronouncing them man and wife.

Since he was only too well aware of the reasons behind this hasty and, to his mind, most ill-considered marriage, the Vicar had not anticipated that immediately upon his pronouncement, the bridegroom would draw his bride into his embrace and press a kiss upon her lips. Indeed, he was quite shocked. No doubt his sense of propriety would have been restored had he been able to hear the exchange between the newly married pair, once they had emerged from the church.

"I hope, my dear," Mr. Bidewell said apologetically "that you did not consider my action untoward, but I thought it might have been expected."

Bryony, her lips still soft and tingling from what she would not have hesitated to describe as a delicious sensation, felt a throb in the region of her heart and was quick to diagnose it as disappointment. She said in a tight little voice, "No, I must agree, Mr. Bidewell. Everyone would have expected it." It did occur to her that since "everyone" included only her Cousins Anne and Hyperion Seton, this statement was not entirely accurate, but she forbore to mention that. Blushing slightly, she added "I do thank you for your . . . assistance."

"I am very glad that I was able to be of service," he said with a constrained smile and with a formality which chilled her. Though, she reminded herself, she had no right to expect anything else. After all, this wedding had originated not in heaven but in her own mind, and it had been instigated for a purpose. That, at least, had been accomplished. From this day forward, Sir Stephen had lost all claim to her person and her property. Then with a slight shiver, she wondered what his reaction might be. She had given scant thought to that. No doubt he would be both angry and hurt. However, as a gentleman, he must take his dismissal philosophically. After all, she thought triumphantly, there was nothing else he could do. The knot was tied!

EIGHT

Sound—screaming, howling, yelling—coupled with the incessant, jarring roars from the cannon, filled his ears. Dazedly he watched the powder boys hurrying across the heaving deck, awash now with seawater turned red with the blood pouring from the jagged wounds of those hapless men who lay near him in that portion of the ship so aptly nicknamed "the slaughterhouse." Just a few feet to his left, Cully Blake, a lad of seventeen years, muttered prayers as he stared unbelievingly at the bloody red stump which had been his right leg. Another man, his arm shot off at the shoulder, screamed and screamed. He, who was still recovering from the flogging that had cut his back to ribbons, had been felled by a falling piece of timber as he had tried to aid some of the wounded. As he wiped the blood from his head, he muttered "Stephen Bardine, Stephen Bardine, Stephen Bardine . . ." and knew that the name was the invocation that would heal his injuries, keep him alive, and aid him to wreak his vengeance. He pressed his hand against his throbbing head and knew that that pain must eventually stop—his back, though hurtful, was better than it had been when they had cut him down—all agony stopped eventually. He had learned that much since he had awakened to the horror of the *Eagle.* Sea water splashed against him. He grimaced. Once he had been desperately afraid of it—no longer. Another blast rocked the ship . . . it might be going down, but no matter, he would survive. . . . "Stephen Bardine . . . Stephen Bardine . . . Stephen Bardine . . ." Bardine would keep him alive.

"Stephen Bardine, I am alive. . . ." He moved restlessly and was confused. Instead of the hard, wet deck beneath his half-naked body, he felt soft linens and opened his eyes to the wide expanse of his bed with its patterned brocade curtains. Coming into focus were dark blue walls hung with numerous paintings, including one of his first Cousin Honoria, as she had looked when she was married to Sir Anthony de Beaufre. His eyes slipped past her pink-and-white loveliness to the full length portrait of dark-browed Sir Anthony, dressed in hunting attire, his hand resting on the head of Cadmus, his favorite wolfhound. Then there was the fireplace with its magnificent white marble mantel, imported from Florence by Sir Anthony's father and upon it, one of the late Baronet's Cellini cups—a lovely ornament, a shell balanced delicately upon the golden tail of a Triton. There had been a time when Mr. Lucas Bardine had hoped to start a similar collection. He had acquired one Cellini, and it must still be at the Court. Directly across the room were the tall windows facing the Park; beyond them it was possible to discern the twin towers of his old home, touched now with the first rays of the rising sun.

He sat up against the padded silken headboard and smiled grimly. His vision still hovered in the back of his mind. In the last five days, he had been mightily plagued by dreams—all much at variance with the luxury of his chamber. His smile vanished, his hands knotted into fists, and the breath he expelled was heavy with strain and frustration. The situation into which he had been catapulted was becoming more and more complicated. When he had agreed to protect Bryony, his mood had been one of exhilaration. In renouncing his plan to use her as a means to approach Sir Stephen Bardine, he had thought himself stalemated; instead, he had been presented with a glorious alternative and one that did much to assuage any lingering pangs of conscience. It was at her suggestion that he was there and it remained only to encounter an angered Sir Stephen, who must surely call him out. As the challenged, he would have his choice of weapons. Pistols or swords? Pistols, he decided after a moment. The business would be done the more quickly—and no nonsense about the seconds stopping the affair at first blood.

He had expected that this confrontation must take place immediately upon returning to the Abbey. If he had been thinking clearly, he would have known that it would not have happened that way. A mirthless smile twisted his lips. According to Thomas, who had passed the word to Mary, Bryony's maid, Sir Stephen was in France and it was not known when he intended to return.

Thus in the last five days, Mr. Bidewell had been compelled to concentrate on making the changes in his manner of living commensurate with his position. Because of that knowing and gossiping fraternity below stairs, he and his bride were obliged to present the appearance of a marriage, and he had therefore moved into the master bedroom, divided from Bryony's chamber by a communicating dressing room.

Staring at its door, he tried to tell himself that he had no desire to open it . . . while in his mind's eye he could envision her chamber, with its beautiful, gilded bed or rather, the occupant of that bed. His imagination painted other, even more vivid pictures, which he did not welcome. When he had entered into this pact, he had given scant thought to the emotions which might arise. He had actually believed it would be easy to respect her wishes, to be a husband in name only. It had not occurred to him that, because of that role, he would be forced to take his meals with her, walk with her in the garden, go riding with her in the morning and spend the evening hours talking, playing chess or, as he had last night, reading parts of the manuscript which she had shyly proffered for his perusal. It had been surprisingly well-constructed, well phrased, too. He smiled, remembering her delight at his encouragement. Then his smile vanished as he pondered on the changes in her that only four years had wrought. He had left her a gay young girl, who, while she had decried and even mocked at the popularity she had enjoyed as an Incomparable, had yet taken considerable pleasure in it. He had returned to find a composed and melancholy young woman, who seemed actually estranged from town life, who cleaved to the country and whose novel revealed almost a contempt for the balls, routs and assemblies in which most females of her age reveled.

He preferred this Bryony but he was not altogether pleased at the reasons for this transformation. He did not hesitate to ascribe them to the hero of her work—the handsome, brooding, nature loving Lord Chadderton-Cleave, who was undoubtedly an idealization of the man she had loved—the man who had died. She had looked most unhappy when he had asked her on whom Chadderton-Cleave was based, though she had denied that he was other than a figment of an imagination fed on the works of Byron, Fanny Burney, Samuel Richardson, and Mrs. Radcliffe. He had not believed her. He had been actively jealous of this man who dwelt only in the pages of that half-finished work. He had been glad that his counterpart was dead. There was no good assuring himself that he did not care for her. Ironically enough he was in the same position that he had been all of his life—he was her dear and respected friend and nothing else. Perhaps in time . . . But he dared not, he would not contemplate that. He had come back to kill Sir Stephen Bardine and take his rightful place at the Court!

His eyes widened and he gripped the sheets. It suddenly came upon him that even with Stephen gone, it might be difficult to assert that claim. Bryony could uphold it, but how could he explain why he had not revealed himself in the first place? His original excuse had been her engagement to Stephen, but she had begged him to save her from that and he had obliged. He should have revealed himself then. How could he make her understand that, because he had been so concentrated upon revenge, he had not wanted his name cleared until he had destroyed his enemy? If she had spoken for him, he might have been denied that opportunity. His original intent had remained unchanged—he did not want Stephen to suffer civil justice. He wanted to be his judge, his jury and his executioner! He gazed across the Park to those gleaming towers. . . .

Was the Court so important to him, or would it be

enough for him to know that Sir Stephen was vanquished, and at a moment when he had believed himself to be safe and secure?

A little cheeping sound aroused him. Looking at the box which he had placed on the table near the bed, he saw that the owl was stirring. He gave it a piece of beef and touched its downy head gently. It was getting bigger and stronger; soon it would be able to fly away. He wondered what its reception might be once it had winged back to the fir tree. He hoped it would not be rejected. It was important to be back among your own . . . his smile was twisted . . . sometimes.

The rose gardens of the Abbey had been planned by the lady of that De Beaufre who had razed the original buildings. They lay in a space surrounded by clipped hedges and further bordered by a low stone wall. The plots themselves, neatly geometrical, were ranged about a fountain centered by a bronze dolphin that sent a stream of crystal water overhead to empty into a wide basin set into a round pool covered with lilypads and stocked with the ubiquitous Japanese goldfish.

On this particular morning it was to be seen that the gardens had benefited greatly from the rains. Many buds had opened into full-blown roses and beyond the stone walls, masses of daffodils and daisies bloomed, while seemingly overnight the trees had become covered with tender green leaves. Though the sun was warm, there was a cool breeze stirring, which caused Miss Seton, who was kneeling by one of the plots to remark, "Look at these petals flutter . . . I vow, these roses do look like butterflies, just as Mr. Soames said they might! Do you not agree, Bryony?"

Bryony glanced at the rose in question, a salmon-colored blossom with only five petals, and said, "Yes, they do have some resemblance." She looked away again. Though she was trying to take an interest in the gardens, she found her attention wandering—well, not exactly wandering, she had to amend. It was actually *traveling* in the direction of the library whither Mr. Bidewell, eschewing their morning ride, had retired immediately upon eating the two pieces of bacon, the slice of toast and the cup of coffee that usually constituted his breakfast; he had, she had noted, a very small appetite for so tall a man. He had not even finished his toast that morning. He had been in a strange, abstracted mood and his decision to work had been expressed in a curt manner that had left her surprised and disappointed—the more so since she had taken particular pains with her appearance, donning a very becoming habit in a blue that matched her eyes and made her hair look more golden than chestnut. She had been very pleased with the image that she had found in her mirror that morning. Though she did not hesitate to ascribe it in part to her release from the betrothal that had weighed so heavily upon her, she was aware that her new relationship with Mr. Bidewell must also be taken into account.

She sighed, hoping that his ill humor was only passing, for she loved their rides, not only because he was an excellent horseman but because she enjoyed being with him, even though he was still distressingly impersonal. Yet it seemed to her that on occasion there had been a look in his eyes which had not been impersonal. She had received enough masculine admiration in her life to recognize it—but had she read more than mere admiration in his gaze or was that only wishful thinking? She asked herself why she should be thinking wishfully about a man who had never addressed one ardent word to her. With a twinge of pain she thought of the two doors that stood between their chambers. Considering the nature of their relationship, it was wrong of her to wish that on some night in the not-too-distant future, she, lying abed, might see one of those portals swing open and . . . She blushed.

Chrissie's confidences were in her ears, and much as she had hated the thought of being with Stephen, she could imagine that had Mr. Bidewell availed himself of the privileges attendant upon their situation . . . But she could not think of that. They had made a pact that he was honorably observing to the letter and she, too, must be . . .

"Bryony—" it was Cousin Anne, sounding a little impatient—"why will you not answer me?"

"I did not hear you. I was thinking. What did you ask me?"

"I wanted to know if you should like to have Mr. Soames put in Portland roses. I have always thought that their color was lovely but of course, it is a matter of taste and in a garden of this size, they might be lost, being shorter than most bushes . . . but scarlet is such a vivid shade and . . ."

"Oh, do as you choose." Bryony shrugged. "I leave the roses to you."

"But dear child, I may not be here to tend them much longer," Miss Seton said.

Bryony stared at her in surprise. "Where might you be going?"

"I . . . had not meant to discuss this topic this morning . . . but I have been thinking that you have no real need of a companion now that you are wed . . ."

"Nonsense," Bryony snapped. "You must certainly stay. Unless you are hinting that you do not approve of Mr. Bidewell?"

"Oh, no, no, no, now that I have seen a little more of him, I find him quite unexceptionable . . . and very well-spoken. I should very much like to remain. I did not mean to interfere, you know. It was only that dear Honoria set such store by Sir Stephen and he being so handsome and so very fond of you . . . then staying out all night, I did feel so responsible, having asked Mr. Bidewell to . . . well, I did not actually ask him, he offered . . . but . . ." She paused, her hand suddenly straying to her bosom, her flickering eyes fixed on a point behind Bryony. "Oh, dear, oh, dear, how came he here and Darby not announcing . . . oh, dear, he does seem extremely put out . . ."

"Whatever is the matter?" Bryony demanded, wondering if her cousin might not have gone mad. Then she was aware of a long shadow falling across the grass and turning swiftly, she saw Sir Stephen Bardine, striding toward them, his face distorted with rage.

Unmindful of the fluttering Miss Seton, who was murmuring little broken words of confusion, he confronted Bryony. "Is it true?" he asked harshly. Before she could respond, he seized her left hand and held it up, glaring at Lady Honoria's wedding ring, which fortunately, he would not recognize, her mother having doffed it when it became too large for her wasted fingers. "Damn you, you little slut, it is true! Why did you do it? Why?"

"Sir Stephen!" Miss Seton stared at him in horror. "How dare you speak to my cousin in such a manner . . . please . . ."

He took no notice of her. Grabbing Bryony's shoulders, he shook her. While the language that poured forth from his mouth was largely incomprehensible to Miss Seton, it sounded dreadful. She picked up her skirts and fled through the gardens into the house. Reaching the library, she slipped inside, her terrified gaze darting about the room. To her chagrin, Mr. Bidewell was not seated in his accustomed perch on the library steps. "Oh, where is he . . ." she murmured distractedly. "I must find him . . . oh, dear . . ."

"Miss Anne." Mr. Bidewell, arising from a large leather chair caused that timorous lady to back up, uttering a cry of fright. He put down the book he had been reading and hurried to her side. "You look very pale—what is amiss?"

"It . . . is in the roses . . . I was showing her the roses," she gabbled. "And Darby, I cannot think why he was so remiss not to announce him, but there is a possibility he came by another way . . . Oh, dear, you must stop him, he is being quite, quite unmannerly. I knew he should be disappointed, but a gentleman . . . such dreadful things as he was saying . . . a slut, he called her . . . a slut and to shake her . . ."

"Stephen!" Mr. Bidewell cried.

She nodded several times. "In the rose gardens . . . the *Rosa chinensis mutabilis* beds, salmon-colored . . . to the left of the fountain . . . butterflies, I always think oh . . ." Her words died on her lips as Mr. Bidewell ran from the room.

Caught in Sir Stephen's iron grip, Bryony struggled to free herself, noting as she did, that his breath was brandy-scented. "Release me immediately!" she commanded furiously. "You are foxed!"

His hold tightened. His fingers pressed into her flesh. "Why . . . why, when we were to be wed next month . . . not even a month . . . three weeks . . . why?" he demanded in choked tones.

"If you heard the story, you know why. I . . . I

thought you'd not want to . . . and I was afraid . . ." Her words trembled into silence before the white-hot fury in his eyes.

"Did he have your maidenhead?" he rasped "Did he ravish you?"

"How dare you!" She flung the words at him. "He . . . he was the soul of honor!"

"Then why did you feel it necessary to marry him!"

"Because no one would have believed me!" she cried.

"*I* would have believed you! Why did you not give me the opportunity to express this belief?" His grasp tightened yet again and he glared into her eyes. "You did not want to marry me. That's the truth of it . . . and you thought you'd found the excuse to cry off, is that it, you conniving little trollop!"

"How dare you speak to me in that manner!" she gasped. "I am not one of the whores with which you must be wont to run and—yes, yes, yes, if you want to know it, that is the truth of it. I did not want to marry you. I never have and would not have even contemplated it had not Mama forced that promise from me!"

"Your mother whom you have betrayed!" he intoned. "Have you no shame . . ."

"You dare talk to me of shame?" she retorted. "I think it must have been you who inveighed upon my poor fond mother to cause her to plead your case . . . Well, there's nothing you can do about it now, Sir Stephen . . . *because I am wed!*"

"Damn you," he grunted. "I should like to break your bloody neck, you . . ." He shook her again so roughly that her teeth slammed against her tongue.

"*That is enough!*" Mr. Bidewell yelled as he came running across the grass with Cousin Anne a few paces behind him. Reaching Sir Stephen, he rounded on him, striking him heavily on the chin and sending him stumbling back among the rosebushes. Stephen was on his feet in an instant, only to be felled a second time.

"I shall not fight you here," his assailant panted. "You may have your seconds call upon me at your will."

"Very well!" Sir Stephen rose slowly, his hand rubbing his chin. "They shall . . . and tomorrow morning at dawn, I will be pleased to cut your damned heart out of your body!"

"And I should be pleased to see you try," Mr. Bidewell responded. "Now get off this land before I summon the footmen and have you thrown off!"

"You . . . you dare threaten me, you nobody from nowhere!" Sir Stephen lunged at him, only to receive a stinging slap across the face.

"If you wish to be in any condition to keep your promise, I suggest that you go now." Mr. Bidewell spoke softly but in a tone of voice that sent shivers through the shocked Bryony. It must have had a very similar effect upon Sir Stephen, for with another glare, he rasped, "You will hear from my seconds." Then, he turned on his heel and strode off through the gardens.

"There," Miss Seton said triumphantly, "he must have come through the Park. There is an opening. Oh, dear, a duel and with swords. Hyperion is much against them . . . not only swords but any weapon. Indeed, though he does not like the French, either, especially the Abbés, whom he feels are very unpriestlike in their demeanor, he is always quoting the one . . . I cannot remember his name, but he said that no war should be fought but with pen and paper. Mr. Bidewell, you must not fight!"

He did not appear to have heard her. His gaze was fastened on Bryony. He was still breathing hard, but slip-

166

ping an arm around her shoulders, he said calmly enough, "Did he hurt you then?"

"No . . . not at all," she cried, her eyes wide with distress. "Orion, you must not fight him! He is deadly with a sword. I can remember two years ago, he fought two duels within three days of each other. One was with a Mr. Crowell; the poor young man nearly died. He is yet an invalid, his lung . . . The other was with a most experienced swordsman . . . he lost his eye. Please, you cannot meet him! I pray that you will not."

The arm that had been encircling her shoulders became very rigid. Releasing her, he stepped back, saying, "Should you expect me to cry off then? Should I send him a carefully-worded note, explaining that it was in the heat of the moment, only, that I struck him, not once but three times, because I could not approve the way he was treating my wife? However, upon further consultation with the lady in question and upon her assurance that she was largely unharmed, I have had second thoughts about my regrettable outburst and pray that he will forgive me for having so far forgotten myself? Perhaps you, as a novelist, would care to help me pen my apology? Might I count on your assistance, my dear—for I am not really sure of how I must phrase it?"

She saw that he had grown very pale and that there was a strange, almost a soulless look in his eyes which reminded her of that which she had seen in the gaze of a captive lion in a London menagerie. Without knowing exactly why, she was frightened by it. "Please . . . I . . . I do not want you to d-demean yourself; but if you meet him, he will kill you and . . ."

"He may kill me—" Mr. Bidewell's words slashed across her protests like a knife—"but there is a chance that he will not. There is a chance that I may kill him."

"I . . . I do not think you have that chance . . . and it is not worth your life . . . Oh God, I never dreamed I should be exposing you to such danger when I asked you to help me! I pray you go . . . go tonight and I shall take all responsibility."

"No, the responsibility is mine, my dear Bree . . . mine alone." Mr. Bidewell spoke softly still, but there was something peculiarly deadly about his intonation. "I have waited for four long years for this opportunity and if you imagine that I shall . . ." He halted suddenly, for she had clutched his wrist and he realized, too late, that his rage had made him careless. He had said too much!

"Bree . . ." She repeated and the name dropped like a rock into the pool of silence that had suddenly come between them. "You . . . called me *Bree.*"

"Is it not short for Bryony?" He tried to speak lightly but he was unsuccessful, his anger being too great for any effort at levity.

"Four years . . . you spoke of four years and you called me 'Bree.' No one in the whole world has ever called me that with the . . . the exception of my Cousin Lucas, who disappeared four years ago." She began to tremble. "He disappeared and was presumed dead."

"What has that to do with me?" he shrugged.

"It will not fadge, Lucas," she whispered. "It is too late for pretenses . . . you *are* Lucas."

"Oh, no, no, no, child, you are beside yourself," Miss Seton, a silent and interested listener to this exchange, said. "Dear Honoria told me that Lucas was . . . well, very heavy and . . ."

"Go away, Cousin Anne," Bryony ordered.

"Go . . . my dear Bryony, what may you mean?" Miss Seton's mouth hung open in shock.

"Leave us at once!" she commanded, actually giving her a push.

Miss Seton, her face a ludicrous mixture of affronted dignity and alarm, scuttled up the path while Bryony stared at him. "You are," she repeated. "I should have guessed it, long ago. There has been so much about you that has reminded me of Lucas."

"You are wrong, I am not . . ." he began, but she was not listening.

"The castle . . . you found it, no one ever has before, but that does not matter. You are Lucas, Lucas, Lucas and nothing you can say will convince me that you are not. But what has happened to you?" Her eyes dwelt on his thin face, "you are so changed! And you spoke of four years . . . four years you have waited for this opportunity, yes, that is what you said. An opportunity to fight Stephen . . . to kill him. What has he done to you? *Tell* me!"

He took a deep breath and then another, "Very well," he said finally, "I expect you have a right to know. In order to cure my fear of the sea, he sent me off on a long ocean voyage . . . to America, aboard the warship *H.M.S. Eagle.* I was one of a number of landsmen impressed for duty aboard her. Most of them perished through ill-treatment, sickness or in battle. I lived."

"Impressed . . . you . . . you were impressed?" she asked incredulously. "But could you not have told them . . ."

"Oh, yes, I told them and had the words thrust back down my gullet by the fist that broke my nose . . . but let me not refine upon my sufferings at sea. Suffice it to say that I survived them."

"And . . . and . . ." She was having trouble in speaking, as question after question piled upon her tongue rising out of a welter of emotions ranging from pity through confusion, grief, and happiness because he was not dead, not dead, not dead. Yet it was all so very strange, so unreal. Finally she managed to blurt out the most important of all those queries, "Stephen did that to you . . . because he coveted your lands, your title . . . ?"

"A most accurate summing up, though I should think that apart from the lands and the title, he coveted you, as well."

"Oh God, why did you not let me know . . . *at once?*"

Meeting her accusing, tear-filled eyes, he tensed. The moment he had been dreading was upon him and he was not ready for it; he had no explanations that could suffice He stared at her almost resentfully. It was not right that he should have been maneuvered into this confrontation at this moment. If he had time to think—he could not think now, not with his knuckles still tingling from their contact with Stephen's chin, and the vengeance for which he had waited so long no more than hours away! There was nothing he could tell her, nothing save the truth that was no longer a truth. "You were betrothed to Stephen and I thought . . ."

"You thought the disappointment might be too great for me to bear, is that it? You thought that I should not be glad that you had returned . . . that I should not fall on my knees and thank God that you had returned, when for four years I had been in torment? Or did you possibly believe that I knew of this terrible plot to defraud you of your possessions . . . was *that* what you believed, Lucas?"

"No, of course it was not, Bree . . ." He put a tentative hand on her shoulder.

She whirled away from him. "Do not touch me!" she

170

cried. "Why did you come here to the Abbey? Why did you not assert your claim and have him arrested? Why this ridiculous masquerade?"

"Why?" he repeated, his own furies rising again. "Who was there left to whom I might appeal? My grandfather was dead and Stephen in residence. My man of business also dead, my staff at the Court disbanded . . . your mother gone. Who would there have been to vouch for me? You were betrothed to Stephen . . . I am sorry, Bree, but I could not trust you. Trusting no longer comes easily to me. I had no papers to prove my identity, no rings, nothing save my word. Nor did I have the money to enlist the services of an advocate; and if I had attempted such a suit, what might have been the result? I am much changed and furthermore, I am marked in a way that could be used to my disadvantage."

"Marked?" she repeated blankly.

"Thus!" he rasped. With fingers that trembled from rage, he ripped open his shirt. "Look . . ." he pointed to the tattoo. "That is registered in the Muster Book of the *Eagle*. It identifies me as one Lemuel Kane, able seaman, and no doubt Stephen or his uncle, Oliver Platt, whose handiwork this is, could produce witnesses to prove that I did indeed serve aboard the *Eagle* and others could assert that I was one of the *Aurora*'s crew, the merchantman on which I earned my passage home. It is far easier for me to prove my identity as Lemuel Kane than as Lucas Bardine!"

"Oh, my God, my God, how dreadful . . . how much you must have suffered . . . that Stephen could have done so horrible a thing and his uncle . . ." She paused. "Platt, you said? Oliver Platt. I know that name—it is the name of Stephen's head groom, a rough looking man, whom I have never liked."

"So that is where he is," he said grimly. "I can well imagine that a gentleman in Stephen's position would not care to acknowledge that relationship, but Platt is his uncle, nonetheless." He touched his chest. "And this was a favor he did for his nephew. So many people have done favors for Stephen Bardine. I being one of them and your mother another, when she wrested that promise from you. Well, my dear, we may both be revenged and upon Stephen, for it is my resolve to return that favor and send him to the hell where he belongs!"

Tears were rolling down her cheeks. "If you had only come to me . . . but I keep forgetting. You said you could not trust me. No, you said more than that. In essence, you suggested I should betray you. You believed that of me, whom you'd known all your life . . . how could you, Lucas, when we've always been so close?"

"I'd thought us close, but then you gave me cause to doubt it. I expect you'd not remember and . . ."

"I do remember . . . I remember everything that has ever passed between us. I remember, too, how I tried to convince you that I'd not meant it as it sounded . . . but what can it matter now? I am so confused. I grant you, I am willing to concede you had reason not to trust me when you found me betrothed to Stephen, though you should have known . . . but considering all you'd undergone, I can find it in my heart not to blame you. Yet, when I told you I hated him . . . when you know that I proposed marrying you to free myself from him . . . why did you not speak then? Why did you let . . ."

"The deception stand when I had the means to prove my case? I did not want to prove it in that manner. I wanted him to call me out as I thought he must when he learned of our marriage!"

"Our marriage . . ." Her eyes flashed. "And I believed you so protective . . . and you married me only for that!" She put her hand to her breast, as if she had experienced a sudden pain.

"Not . . . only . . . because of that," he said haltingly. "I was sorry for you . . . I did want to help you, but yes, there was also my . . . plan. Think hardly of me if you will. I might have spared you all this, but for my own peace of mind, I could not. I came here to kill him—"

"Supposing he kills you!" she cried. "You were never a fighter, Lucas. What can you know of swords and pistols?"

"I have learned much in the past four years," he said grimly. "Stephen will find me an opponent worthy of his mettle."

"Oh, Lucas," she sobbed, "you cannot fight him. Forget this revenge. It is not worthy of you. Is it not revenge enough to deprive him of all he holds most dear —his so-called position at the Court, his title . . . we could institute criminal proceedings against him. He could be transported! Would that not satisfy you?"

"Nothing will satisfy me save his blood on my hands."

Staring at his set features, she shuddered. "No, you must not say that." She moved to him and grasped his arms, looking up at him pleadingly. "Lucas, if you persist in this . . . endeavor, you'll be the loser, not Stephen, no, not even if you do kill him! Such hatred corrodes and warps the soul!"

"So be it," he returned coldly. Then pausing, he added in a softer voice, "You must not think that I do not appreciate all you are saying, Bryony. You are more than magnanimous to want to be my friend after I have deceived you and used you . . ."

"I am not your friend," she contradicted hotly. "A

mere friend might have hated you for what you have done, but I cannot hate you, not when I have loved you all my life and love you still. It is because I love you that I cannot bear to see you destroy yourself!"

"Because you love me?" he repeated in disbelief. "And what of the man who died?"

"That man is you!" she cried. "Oh, Lucas, Lucas, come with me to London . . . come tonight and we will begin proceedings against him. I beg you will come with me. It is madness to fight him!"

He pulled away from her, "It may be madness, perhaps it is, but I cannot forgo it, Bryony, I cannot. I have lived for this moment."

She was silent then, staring at him. In a low trembling voice, she said, "You are wrong, Lucas. You have not lived for this moment, you have died for it. The Lucas Bardine I knew and loved is dead." With a choking sob, she turned and ran swiftly from the garden.

He stared after her. He had an impulse to follow her, but ruthlessly he downed it, cresting the wave of debilitating emotion that threatened to sweep away his purpose. She did not matter. Nothing mattered save that meeting which must and would take place upon the morrow.

Not quite as he had planned, though. Rather than provoking Stephen's challenge, he had, in the heat of their strife, offered his own—and Sir Stephen Bardine, master swordsman, had exercised his right as the challenged party to choose his weapon. It would not be the quick business Lucas had meant it to be . . . but, win or lose, Stephen Bardine would confront an avenging fury at dawn.

NINE

Bryony, huddled in a chair pulled close to her bedroom windows, had watched the sunset-painted clouds darken and disappear with the coming of night. She had seen the night brighten under the rising moon and dim with its descent. Now the sky was dark grey, though at the horizon its color was paling. In her mind's eye, she could see that stretch of level ground that lay beyond the boundaries of the town and which was known as Chalmer's Glade. Many duels had been fought in that spot; there was even a legend to the effect that the numerous species of wildflowers that covered it during the spring owed their brilliant colors to the human blood that had nourished their roots. It was spring now and before the sun rose more blood would have seeped into those thirsty roots.

She shuddered but she did not weep. Her tears were spent. Her whole body felt empty, drained of emotion. She wondered where Lucas was now? In the middle of the afternoon, young Jeffrey Ingram, the scion of a neighboring family and one of Stephen's few friends, had come to call on Lucas to arrange the hour and the place of the meeting, information duly communicated to her by an excited and frightened Mary, who had had it from Thomas, the groom, who was, amazingly, acting as Lucas's second. After Mr. Ingram's departure, Lucas had gone from the house, nor had he returned that night. Where had he slept, if he had slept? Or had he walked up and down as she herself had done, pacing the floor of her chamber, her mind weighted with the knowledge that had come to her that day. There had been moments when she had almost succeeded in hating him, but these had not lasted.

Oddly enough, in the long, long hours which had passed so slowly—but not slowly enough, for it was nearly morning and the time of the meeting fast approaching —she could think only of his hands, those hard, ruined hands with their calloused palms, scarred backs and smashed nails. She had contrasted them with the plump, white, soft, and beautifully manicured hands which Lucas Bardine had once used with such grace. More than his words, more than that horrid tattoo on his chest, his hands told the story of the last four years; and, thinking of his prolonged ordeal, her nails bit into her palms and she could understand . . . Yes, she could understand why he should crave vengeance, could understand why he would resort to any means to achieve it, could even forgive him for the cruel deception he had practiced upon her.

Yet . . . to fight Stephen Bardine? Despite his assurances she was frightened for him. Stephen had a cruel streak. It was evidenced not only by what he had done to

Lucas but by the pleasure he took in mills, in cockfights and bearbaitings. She had no doubt that he had enjoyed those duels as well. He had not been angry enough to slay his opponents, but given his present thwarted fury he would be a formidable—a deadly foe.

Lucas, notwithstanding his rage, was not a born fighter. There was too much kindliness in his nature. Yes, even now, he had proved that when he had rescued the owl. She remembered how tenderly he had cosseted it. She also rememberd their old animal hostel and his hatred of hunting and trapping. He was no match for Stephen!

She smote her hands together. It was not fair, not right that the man who had done him so terrible an injury must also kill him! Something had to be done to stop the duel—but nothing could be done. For the greater part of the night, she had endeavored to evolve some manner of stratagem that might prevent the meeting taking place. She had been unsuccessful. If only she might prevail upon the Earl of Ranfully, who was Justice of Peace for the district . . . but that was impossible. He was known to be ill and had been for the last three months She could not, she knew, call upon a constable, for none would take it on himself to step upon a field of honor involving the master of Bardine Court. Yet if she herself might interfere . . . but how? Outside of shooting Stephen, she could do nothing.

Her eyes narrowed. Back of them, she was seeing her father shooting at a target set up in the lower gardens. It had been his contention that one was compelled to take the field at least two or three times in one's life—'or, as he had said with a grim laugh, "any chancy remark might occasion a duel." He had in fact, once been called out for complaining because a man sitting behind him at Drury Lane was talking so loudly that he could not hear the actors.

"It is better," he had said to the admiring little girl who had stood watching him, "to eat the wolf than to have the wolf eat you." Then because she had plaintively demanded to be allowed to shoot at that target, too, he had given her one of the pistols, showed her how to load it, cock it and shoot it.

It had been a lesson that had horrified Lady Honoria and, out of deference to her wishes, it had not been repeated; but Bryony could still recall the feel of the pistol, cold against her fingers. She could remember, too, that she had hit the target close enough to its dark center to surprise and please her father. She had done it several times before her mother had come running. Those pistols were in a drawer of the library desk!

She looked out of the window. The sky was paling. Soon it would be time, and she knew what she must do —she would take one of the pistols and go to the dueling ground. If Stephen showed signs of winning, she would shoot him—no matter what the consequences! Lucas must not be killed.

The chill of dawn was in the air and the grass heavy with dew. Thomas Jenkins, a stocky, fair-haired youth of twenty, shifted his feet, wishing he had not stepped into the long grass that edged the bare stretch of ground where the duel was soon to take place. His feet felt uncomfortably wet, but that sensation was less uncomfortable than the embarrassment he was experiencing as he stood near Jeffrey Ingram, his fellow-second. Ingram, some two years his senior, was further separated from him by a gulf of birth and breeding. It was obvious from his haughty affronted stare that he had not expected to be allied with a mere groom. It was also obvious to Thomas that Ingram's contempt embraced Mr. Bidewell, who was standing nearby, testing the slim rapier that was of his opponent's providing. The groom's eyes flickered past Mr. Ingram to rest on Sir Stephen Bardine, of whom the members of his household were not fond. According to the butler, who was an especial crony of Thomas's, he was a penny-pinching master, who stuck his long nose into the kitchens, the pantries, the stables, and all other parts of the house and grounds which were the proper domain of the housekeeper, butler, footmen, and grooms, querying expenditures and examining receipts in a manner oddly at variance from that of most of the Quality. Though none of the staff had been there in the days of the late Mr. Lucas Bardine, the word about the town was that he knew how to treat his servants and had been a singularly liberal, kindly man, whom everybody at the Court had respected.

Thomas shot a look at the horses and saw Mr. Oliver Platt, the head groom. It was said that he was on far too familiar terms with his master. Indeed, it was a wonder that he was not standing in the place of Mr. Jeffrey Ingram. Thomas was glad that he was where he ought to be. He did not care for Mr. Platt, who was a strange mixture of obsequiousness and arrogance and who never mingled with his fellow servants. Watching him now, he saw he was scowling, an expression that did not enhance his battered features. He was nearly as ugly as the pit bull kept by old Smithers, the hostler at the Crown and Scepter. In fact, he did not look unlike the cur.

Thomas, shifting his gaze to Sir Stephen, found the look on his face equally unprepossessing. Though he was handsome, there was a twist to his mouth and a narrowness to his eyes that fair gave Thomas the shivers. He was put in mind of a murderer he had once seen being led off to his execution. Of course—and here Thomas firmed his lips to conceal a grin—he must be in a fair fury for, from all accounts, he had been mightily disappointed what with Miss Bryony going off and wedding Mr. Bidewell after that night in the woods!

Thomas would have given a monkey to know what had transpired between them, though Mary had been sure that nothing untoward had happened. However, they *had* spent a whole night together, had they not?—and though Mr. Bidewell for all he was soft-spoken and scholarly, with a way about him that put him securely among the Quality, was still a man who had a fair amount of red blood in his veins. Thomas could only hope that he might not see some of that red blood staining Mr. Bidewell's white shirt soon. He winced. He could not understand the penchant the Quality had for settling quarrels with the sword or the gun, when fists were just as good and you did not stand to lose your life. He glanced at the doctor and saw that he was looking most disapproving. It was well known that Dr. Metcalf, who was young and new to these parts, did not hold with dueling, and right he was.

"My good man." Mr. Ingram stepped to his side, saying in his persnickety tones, "They are ready. I shall call 'On Guard', if it meets with your approval?"

"That it does," Thomas said, wishing heartily that he had the authority to stop the match. Though Mr. Bidewell was tall and muscular and though from his expression, he was seething with rage, he was not sorry that the bet he had laid on the outcome of the encounter had been in Sir Stephen's favor.

Much to Bryony's chagrin, the signal had been given and the duel was in progress when she arrived. That was because she had been delayed. On coming out of the library, she had met Cousin Anne, clad in a long trailing gown, apologizing for her deshabille and gabbling that she could not sleep for thinking of Lucas Bardine and Stephen's perfidy, Bryony having informed her as to the whole of it. The idea of the duel had been particularly abhorrent to Miss Seton.

"It should not be allowed . . . it ought to be stopped . . . a Justice of the Peace . . ." she had said vaguely.

"Ranfully is the only one we could ask," Bryony had returned impatiently, "and you know he is ill."

"But surely . . ." Miss Seton had protested.

"I must go," Bryony had told her firmly. She had not managed to escape as quickly as she would have liked, for she had had to make up an excuse as to why she was dressed for riding. Certainly she had not dared to incite an argument by telling her cousin of her destination. She was heartily glad that she had concealed the pistol in the pocket of her cloak before emerging from the library.

She had encountered another delay in the stables, for Joseph, the second groom, had not handled Albion with the expertise of Thomas, and the animal had retaliated with some very skittish behavior. He had acted up again when she had dismounted, making it difficult to tie him to a tree. She prayed that Mr. Platt, who was standing at the far end of the glade with the other horses, had not seen her arrive. She did not think he had noticed, for he was watching the proceedings on the field most intently. She was glad of the trees. Though they were still sparsely leafed, they grew very close together and she was able to slip from trunk to trunk until she was at the edge of the field, stationed behind the wide trunk of an ancient oak. Since she was only a few feet away from the duelists she had a fine view of what was taking place. She slid her hand into her pocket and brought out the pistol, holding it in readiness. But because of what she feared might be her overzealous trigger finger, she set it only at half-cock.

She watched tensely. The two men were very well-matched, she thought desolately, wishing that Lucas had had the advantage. Actually, Lucas appeared more power-fully built than his cousin. It was incredible that this slim man had once been so heavy and lumbering. There was nothing lumbering about his movements now—he was grace itself and, to her great relief, he did handle his sword well, neatly parrying Stephen's fierce lunges. How-ever, it was obvious to her that neither man was making any progress and the clash of steel on steel seemed to go on interminably. Then suddenly her attention was di-verted. She had heard the sound of carriage wheels!

Glancing to her right, she saw that a carriage had stopped at the edge of the Glade and that an old man was being assisted from it. Her eyes widened—as he moved closer, she recognized the Earl of Ranfully and behind him her Cousin Anne! Her heart leaped. He had come to stop the duel! She looked toward the duelists and then bit back a cry for in that very second, Stephen's sword had slid under his opponent's guard and, though Lucas moved back, the blade had slit open his shirt.

Bryony stepped forward. She did not even think of her pistol. How seriously had he been wounded? There were red marks on his chest—but, she realised they were the garish markings of the tattoo, not blood—and mean-while his blade had come smashing down on Stephen's sword. Stephen staggered back, his eyes on Lucas's exposed chest, his face as white as his shirt. He cried shrilly, "Lucas . . . Lucas Bardine, *you are Lucas Bardine!*"

Bryony was vaguely aware that the Earl had come closer and that Jeffrey Ingram was stepping forward. Then Lucas panted, "Yes, Cousin Stephen, as you say—I am Lucas Bardine." So saying, he thrust in *quatre,* his sword driving through Stephen's suddenly relaxed guard and aiming at his heart. Yet as his opponent's death seemed imminent, with a flick of his wrist Lucas ran his cousin through the shoulder and stepped back. Stephen, glaring at him, lifted his sword arm and then dropped it, collapsing at his feet.

"Lucas!" Bryony mouthed, her voice shock-stilled in her throat, knowing that he had acted true to form, knowing that though he had had Stephen Bardine at his mercy, he could never have pursued his course to its inevitable end. Stephen was alive, and could not have been wounded very seriously, for though he was groaning, he was also cursing. She was about to run to Lucas, when her arm was seized and the pistol wrenched from her grasp.

Whirling around she saw Mr. Platt clutching it, his face pale and his eyes murderous. In a second he had pointed the pistol at Lucas, who stood staring down at his fallen cousin. Bryony sprang toward Lucas, negotiating the small space between them in a single bound and flinging herself against him. She cried, "Look out . . . look out, he will shoot!" Even as she spoke, there was a loud report and she felt a searing pain in her upper arm.

"Bree . . . Bree!" Lucas clutched her.

"It was my fault . . ." she gasped. "My p-pistol and I thought to . . . to help you, but he . . . oh, my arm . . ." She sagged against him.

"Bree, my love, my dearest, oh God!" to his horro
he saw a spreading stain of red on her sleeve.

His voice was faint in her ears and she was gla
when he eased her to the ground. For all that her di
ziness had lasted but a moment, her arm pained her, an
it was pleasant to be lying down, now that she knew th
duel was over and Lucas safe. She tried to protest whe
he ripped her habit from her shoulder, easing it gentl
down her arm, but then her attention was diverted by th
Earl of Ranfully's acerbic tones, mingled with Cousi
Anne's affrighted murmurs and Stephen's groans. Top
ping these was Thomas's exultant shout that he ha
brought down Mr. Platt. That was extremely satisfyin
Even more satisfying were Lucas's anguished words: "O
my God, Bree, how could you endanger your life fc
me . . . how could you?"

She tried to sit up. "I love you," she murmured as
that were all the explanation he needed.

"And I love you . . . oh God, if you had died,
should not have wanted to live!"

She reached up with her good arm and touched h
cheek. "I am so proud of you, Lucas . . . so proud yo
acted as I had hoped . . . as I knew you must and . . ."

"Shhh," he begged, "you must not talk. Your poc
arm . . ."

"I do not talk with my arm," she said in stronge
accents. Smiling mistily, she pushed a dark lock of ha
back from his forehead. "Oh, Lucas, my own darling, yo
have come back to me at last. I have missed you so dreac
fully."

She might have said much more in that same vei
had he not enfolded her in an embrace so crushing tha
once she had recovered from the ecstasy of his kiss, sh

did need to remind him that her arm was a little sore; only to have him kiss that injured limb. Until the doctor, having tended Stephen, ordered Lucas away and bandaging what he described as a mere scratch, consigned Byrony to her husband's care again.

An hour later, Bryony, lying on her bed, with Lucas sitting beside her, looked meekly at the Earl of Ranfully, who faced her from a deep arm chair. Pounding his stick on the floor, he said. "I do not believe in violence . . . the idea of bringing that pistol with you!"

"You must excuse her, my Lord," Miss Seton, ensconced on a bench by the wall, murmured. "She could not have been thinking clearly."

"It is true . . . I was not . . . I only wanted to save Lucas. . . ."

"Very worthy," growled the Earl. "However, neither of you was thinking clearly." He glared at Lucas. "If you had come to me in the very beginning that rascal and his uncle would have been in chains! My God, I'd have had no trouble in recognizing you. You're the very spit of Sir Bertram at your age. Why did you not come?"

Lucas flushed. "I . . . uh . . ."

"You forgot I existed, no doubt," the Earl rasped. "Well, no matter, it's all right and tight now and Mr. Platt in gaol where he ought to be and when his nephew recovers, he'll be joining him. You know, you could have that pair hanged."

"No," Lucas said, "I do not want that. Indeed, my Lord, I am satisfied . . ."

"You're not thinking of freeing them!" Bryony gasped.

"Wouldn't do him any good if he were," the Earl told

her. "They are under arrest and no one can interfere with the due process of law. We'll have 'em up before the next Assizes and it's my guess they'll be transported."

"Which is as it should be," Bryony said.

"Oh, yes, yes," Miss Seton breathed. "So very dastardly . . . to despoil poor Sir Lucas . . ."

"I quite agree," the Earl broke in. "On Monday next we shall make arrangements for the transfer of the title, Sir Lucas, and you should be in possession of the Court before too much longer."

Lucas's eyes lighted. "I do thank you, my Lord."

The Earl rose, "No need to thank me. I am only sorry it could not have been done sooner. That was your fault, young man."

"I acknowledge it, sir," Lucas said. "I shall see you out."

"No." The Earl looked at Bryony. "Miss Seton must oblige. It is the least she can do, waking me from a deep sleep and at dawn. Come, Miss Anne, and on the way I shall expect you to show me some of your famous roses."

"Oh, how have you heard about those?" Miss Seton marveled.

"Gardeners talk. Mine is envious of your green thumb."

"Oh, it has nothing to do with me," she assured him. "The soil is excellent and bones help . . ."

"Bones?" The Earl looked at her perplexedly as he opened the door for her.

"Fertilizer . . . it is much better than—" she flushed suddenly—"than *other* sorts of fertilizer and . . ." She was out of the room and the Earl, stumping after her, actually winked as he closed the door behind them.

"Oh, Lucas," Bryony murmured, "isn't it lovely . . .?"

"Lovely," he agreed, coming to sit beside her on the bed and kiss her.

"But," she said a minute later, "you could not have meant that you wanted to have Stephen and Mr. Platt pardoned!"

"I thought you did not approve of revenge," he countered.

"I do not approve of soul-searing vengeance, but I do believe in the laws." Her jaw set. "I want him to suffer. I hope that he is transported and put into one of those gangs that work on the roads. I understand that it is very hard labor indeed."

"So vindictive," he murmured. "I, on the other hand, think we must be thankful to my wicked cousin—"

"Thankful!" She glared at him. "I shall not allow you to be *that* magnanimous. Why would we thank him?"

"Because he brought us together. Lucas Bardine as he was four years ago would never have dared aspire to the hand of the beautiful—the Incomparable, Miss Bryony de Beaufre."

"Had the said Mr. Lucas Bardine not offered, I should have," she said staunchly. "In fact, Mr. Orion Bidewell, if you will remember, I *did*. However, I do not happen to think of Mr. Stephen Bardine as my wicked cousin."

"Ah—" he kissed her ear—" then you have forgiven him?"

"Never in a million billion years!" She glared at him. "But *you*, my love, are the wicked cousin for not having trusted me right from the beginning and . . . oh!" She flushed, for Mr. Bardine had suddenly stretched out on the bed beside her and taken her into his arms, a purposeful look in his eye.

187

Some time later, Bryony, lifting her head from her husband's bare chest, reached over to touch the V on his arm. "What does this mean?" she murmured jealously, "Virginia . . . Venetia . . ."

"Vision," he corrected.

"A vision of what?" she demanded, looking at him in a puzzled way.

"Of you, my own beloved. For I can scarce believe that you are real."

"I thought," Bryony smiled, "that I had proved that . . . beyond all possible doubt."

ROMANCE...ADVENTURE...
DANGER...

THIS TOWERING PASSION
by Valerie Sherwood   **(81-486, $2.50)**
500 pages of sweet romance and savage adventure set against the violent tapestry of Cromwellian England, with a magnificent heroine whose beauty and ingenuity captivates every man who sees her, from the king of the land to the dashing young rakehell whose destiny is love!

THIS LOVING TORMENT
by Valerie Sherwood   **(82-649, $2.25)**
Born in poverty in the aftermath of the Great London Fire, Charity Woodstock grew up to set the men of three continents ablaze with passion! The bestselling sensation of the year, boasting 1.3 million copies in print after just one month, to make it the fastest-selling historical romance in Warner Books history!

THESE GOLDEN PLEASURES
by Valerie Sherwood   **(82-416, $2.25)**
From the stately mansions of the east to the freezing hell of the Klondike, beautiful Rosanne Rossiter went after what she wanted —and got it all! By the author of the phenomenally successful THIS LOVING TORMENT.

LOVE'S TENDER FURY
by Jennifer Wilde   **(81-909, $2.50)**
The turbulent story of an English beauty—sold at auction like a slave—who scandalized the New World by enslaving her masters. She would conquer them all—only if she could subdue the hot unruly passions of the heart! The 2 Million Copy Bestseller that brought fame to the author of DARE TO LOVE.

DARE TO LOVE
by Jennifer Wilde   **(81-826, $2.50)**
Who dared to love Elena Lopez? She was the Queen of desire and the slave of passion, traveling the world—London, Paris, San Francisco—and taking love where she found it! Elena Lopez— the tantalizing, beautiful moth—dancing out of the shadows, warmed, lured and consumed by the heart's devouring flame.

LILIANE
by Annabel Erwin   **(91-219, $2.50)**
The bestselling romantic novel of a beautiful, vulnerable woman torn between two brothers, played against the colorful background of plantation life in Colonial America.

AURIELLE
by Annabel Erwin   **(91-126, $2.50)**
The tempestuous new historical romance 4 million Annabel Erwin fans have been waiting for. Join AURIELLE, the scullery maid with the pride of a Queen as she escapes to America to make her dreams of nobility come true.

THE BEST OF BESTSELLERS
FROM WARNER BOOKS

DESIRE AND DREAMS OF GLORY
by Lydia Lancaster　　　　　　　　　　　　**(81-549, $2.50)**

In this magnificent sequel to Lydia Lancaster's PASSION AND PROUD HEARTS, we follow a new generation of the Beddoes family as the headstrong Andrea comes of age in 1906 and finds herself caught between the old, fine ways of the genteel South and the exciting changes of a new era.

A PASSIONATE GIRL
by Thomas Fleming　　　　　　　　　　　　**(81-654, $2.50)**

The author of the enormously successful LIBERTY TAVERN is back with this gusty and adventurous novel of a young woman fighting in the battle for Ireland's freedom and persecuted for her passionate love of a man.

PHILIPPA
by Katherine Talbot　　　　　　　　　　　　**(84-664, $1.75)**

If she had to marry for money, and Philippa knew she must, then it was fortunate that such a very respectable member of the House of Lords was courting her. It was easy to promise to "honor and obey" a man she so respected. It would be difficult, though, to forget that the man she loved and did not respect would be her brother-in-law . . . A delightful Regency Romance of a lady with her hand promised to one man and her heart lost to another!

LADY BLUE
by Zabrina Faire　　　　　　　　　　　　**(94-056, $1.75)**

A dashing Regency adventure involving a love triangle, an enfant terrible and a bizarre scheme to "haunt" a perfectly livable old castle, LADY BLUE is the story of Meriel, the beautiful governess to an impossible little boy who pours blue ink on her long blonde hair. When she punishes the boy, she is dismissed from her post. But all is not lost—the handsome young Lord Farr has another job in mind for her. Meriel's new position: Resident "ghost" in a castle owned by Farr's rival. Her new name: LADY BLUE!

THE FIVE-MINUTE MARRIAGE
by Joan Aiken　　　　　　　　　　　　**(84-682, $1.75)**

When Delphie Carteret's cousin Garth asks her to marry him, it is in a make-believe ceremony so that Delphie might receive a small portion of her rightful—if usurped—inheritance. But an error has been made. The marriage is binding! Oh, my! Fun and suspense abounds, and there's not a dull moment in this delightful Regency novel brimming with laughter, surprise and true love.

MORE WARNER ROMANCES

MY LADY BENBROOK
by Constance Gluyas   (91-124, $2.50)

The Earl of Benbrook had schooled Angel Dawson well. The street accents were gone from her speech when he presented her as a gracious lady at the court of the King. And Angel had taught Nicholas, too, the lessons of love. They had earned her an even more precious honor; she was now his wife, the Lady Benbrook!

THE KING'S BRAT
by Constance Gluyas   (91-125, $2.50)

The Earl of Benbrook gazed at the waif who had been kind to his dying sister. With a mixture of guilt and gratitude, he vowed to turn the street wench into a lady. It was a task that would involve him with Angel far more deeply than he guessed, and would change her far more than she dreamed! The temptestuous tale of Angel Dawson's rise from the streets of London to the court of Charles II.